Robyn,

I'll Always Love You

SUNSET BEACH STORIES

SHARON HAMILTON WRITING AS
ANNIE CARR

Enjoy!

Annie Carr

SHARON HAMILTON'S BOOK LIST

SEAL BROTHERHOOD BOOKS

SEAL BROTHERHOOD SERIES
Accidental SEAL Book 1
Fallen SEAL Legacy Book 2
SEAL Under Covers Book 3
SEAL The Deal Book 4
Cruisin' For A SEAL Book 5
SEAL My Destiny Book 6
SEAL of My Heart Book 7
Fredo's Dream Book 8
SEAL My Love Book 9
SEAL Encounter Prequel to Book 1
SEAL Endeavor Prequel to Book 2
Ultimate SEAL Collection Vol. 1 Books 1-4 /2 Prequels
Ultimate SEAL Collection Vol. 2 Books 5-7

SEAL BROTHERHOOD LEGACY SERIES
Watery Grave Book 1
Honor The Fallen Book 2
Grave Injustice Book 3
Deal With The Devil Book 4
Cruisin' For Love Book 5
Destiny of Love Book 6
Heart of Gold Book 7

Paradise: In Search of Love
Love Me Tender, Love You Hard

NOVELLAS
SEAL You In My Dreams Magnolias and Moonshine

PARANORMALS

GOLDEN VAMPIRES OF TUSCANY SERIES
Honeymoon Bite Book 1
Mortal Bite Book 2
Christmas Bite Book 3
Midnight Bite Book 4

THE GUARDIANS
Heavenly Lover Book 1
Underworld Lover Book 2
Underworld Queen Book 3
Redemption Book 4

FALL FROM GRACE SERIES
Gideon: Heavenly Fall

SUNSET BEACH SERIES
I'll Always Love You
Back To You

NOVELLAS
SEAL Of Time Trident Legacy

All of Sharon's books are available on Audible,
narrated by the talented J.D. Hart.

ABOUT THE BOOK

Family preparations for a grandmother's 80th birthday party are complicated by the mysterious disappearance of the guest of honor.

A saga of long-lost love, redemption, second chances, and a happily ever after unfolds as each family member plays a part in this passion play. Shocking secrets are revealed and motivations are discovered, binding them all together into a colorful tapestry of duty, love, and honor.

For true love grows in the gardens of the heart, and there's always time for a second chance at love.

AUTHOR'S NOTE

This story is loosely based on a beautiful story I was told several years ago, and I've wanted to write it ever since I heard it. Although I have taken great liberties, changed much of the details and descriptions of the families involved, it is the story of two lovers who found each other after their lives had gone different directions, and lived the last of their years together in a remote cabin. And yes, the family thought their beloved grandma had been kidnapped at first.

And there was a child born, like Maggie, and a husband taken, like Frank.

But all the rest of it is my imagination and artistic embellishment and doesn't resemble the original story, except in the big picture arc of the story.

This has been my first foray into writing Women's Fiction or Sweet Romance works, and I have to say it's been one of the most enjoyable books to write, almost writing itself.

And like my own story, my author penname Annie Carr lives her life at the Florida Gulf Coast, embellishing her own story with more magic to follow. I hope you'll continue on hers and my journey in the years to come.

Can you see the years?

Annie Carr/Sharon Hamilton

February 2023

Chapter 1

Annie Carr

SWEET ROMANCE AUTHOR

"**G**RANNY'S GONE!"

"What do you mean 'gone?'" Faith's mother echoed.

"She's not here. I'm at the Springs Home, and she's not here. They said she left last night. The staff thought she was going to return, but this morning, when she wasn't in her bed, they called me. She's just not here, Mom. She hasn't been here all night."

Faith struggled to breathe, her cheeks puffy and flushed. She gripped her cell phone so tightly she nearly cracked the frame.

Her mother answered her back, her timbre laced with venom and sharp objects. "They called the police, of course?"

"I believe so. Yes. But—"

"And can you explain to me why they didn't call you *last night*? I mean, this could be a kidnapping, an emergency. Have I got this right?"

"I don't know, Mom. But the staff, at least Mr. Gates, says she went with somebody willingly—*a man.*"

"God in Heaven! I never thought that stubborn streak of hers would last into her eighties. She knows we're all here to watch over her. She always did like to go her own way, but this is downright selfish of her, if this was her choice. And I'm not so sure it was. Her behavior is beginning to degrade into complete recklessness. Unless—unless it is a true kidnapping. She must not have been of her right mind. *A man?* She went with a *strange man?*"

Faith heard the tremor in her mother's voice, the panic mirroring her own. She'd been hoping her mother might know something about all of this. Her stomach sunk down to her ankles with the realization that something very bad had happened and she was powerless to do anything about it, after the fact.

"Mom, I'm just trying to sort it out, and I thought I'd let you know right away. You guys going to drive up here, or do you want me to do some more checking around and call you back first?"

Her mother paused and then began again, carefully, "Well, she's been gone overnight, so if she's out in the elements, she could be dead by now, Faith."

That made her freeze, stumbling for something to say but finding nothing. Hearing it out loud made her shake, nearly peeing her pants. The thought of finding her grandmother frozen to death in the woods, drowned at the bottom of a river or lake, fallen down a ravine, or torn apart by bears that roamed the area distracted her. The background chatter coming from her mother's mouth finally caught up to her.

"Oh my God, I can't believe this is happening to us. Did she tell anybody she was planning on a trip or planning to meet someone?"

"The night shift attendant hasn't come in yet. You remember her nurse, Sally? The one she likes. The one who reads her all those sexy books."

"How could I forget? After Frank died, Mom became a collector—had hundreds of those awful things stashed everywhere. The staff from the home would stop by to pick up handfuls. I took them out after we moved her across the hall. She was tripping over them, literally, and it was a fire hazard. They were in boxes and stuffed under the bed in plastic totes like cherished photographs. I even found some in the bathroom cabinets. They'd fall over, and she'd trip over them when she got out of bed. I was worried she'd break her hip. She didn't hoard anything else in her life, but she hoarded those romance novels like crazy. I didn't have the heart to tell her they all went to the used bookstore when she asked me."

"I remember. But I think she'd be okay with that. She lent them to her friends all the time. The main thing is we've got to find out where *she* went. And if she left with someone, I've got to think they'd be staying somewhere nearby, perhaps in his house. Maybe she made some new friends or maybe this is the beginning of Alzheimer's. She could be forgetting where she is or who she is or where she lives. Maybe she thought she was going home. Should I go drive by her old house?"

"You need to wait there until the police come, and then after the report's been filed and you've exhausted everything, yeah, I'd go over to the house and just check things out. Talk to the neighbors—find out if somebody has seen her. There's nobody living there now, and the water is disconnected. We're in between tenants. But maybe she thought she still lived there and went to spend the night. We didn't put furniture covers on anything, so it is probably all dusty and full of mice. The heat's turned off. It wouldn't be a place she'd want to stay."

Faith heard her mother sob.

"This is the worst thing in the world. And here we are celebrating, putting together this birthday party for her, and she takes off. Do you suppose she was embarrassed or somehow offended that we were doing this? You know she can be funny about certain things."

"Oh, Mom, no way. She had a bright smile on her face every time we talked about it. She was so looking forward to it."

"Maybe there's some kind of an undiagnosed condition, a mental condition."

"Mom, I think we must get ready for what's coming up next for her. We find her first, and then we'll have her evaluated. There are places for memory care. Maybe she'll have to go to one of those."

"But she wanted to stay in the home where Frank was. We could have gotten her home care, but she insisted she stay there with him. I almost feel like he's standing right next to me here giving me a lecture about not taking care of his wife. All the way from the grave, he's directing us, telling us what to do."

"Yup, that was Grandpa."

"He was always the one everybody deferred to, including Mom. Maybe she thought she was meeting him? What do you think?"

"I have no clue. I'm sorry. I had no warning whatsoever."

After Faith hung up from her mother, she interviewed several staff. Dr. Craven, who took over her grandfather's country practice when he retired, still visited every single one of his elderly charges in rest homes all over Tennessee, at least once a week. He was making the rounds today and stopped her in the hallway.

"I just heard about your grandmother. She never mentioned a trip when I saw her last week. She seemed perfectly lucid too."

"My mom wants to know if maybe she was anxious or had second thoughts about the big birthday party we were planning?"

"Why no. It was actually quite the opposite," he said. "I'm trying to think what we talked about last time. She was going to get her hair done, and she had contracted with one of the staff to take her shopping for a new dress. Yes—she wanted a new dress and a new pair of shoes. Some comfortable ones. She said she wanted to dance at her 80th birthday party."

Faith smiled as her heart warmed. She had so many fond memories of her grandmother, who always took a special interest in her even though she had five other grandchildren.

She added, "Every time I talked to her, she wanted to know what we were doing, who had RSVP'd, what the menu was going to be, and if there were any changes. She seemed to be really into it. She even asked me if she should write a personal invite to a few people or call them."

"That's exactly as I remember it. She was all over my case for me and the missus to attend. I told her I would drop by—I promised her that. But this, this really throws me, Faith. It must have been something important or, and I hate to think of it, maybe she had a little stroke or memory lapse and got talking to some stranger and one thing led to another and—well, you know. Beersheba Springs is a small town, so I hope it's not going to take them very long to locate her. I wouldn't worry about it, except for the fact that she's been gone all night. But she did leave with someone else, and let's hope not under any nefarious circumstances or with ill intent. That's what I'm going to focus on."

Although she appreciated Dr. Craven's optimism, it didn't do anything to ease her nerves. She conceded defeat. "The head nurse reported she seemed to go willingly." Then Faith remembered one extra detail. "Actually, she said Granny had packed a bag."

"You mean a suitcase?"

"No, she said it was her knitting bag, the big huge thing that she liked to carry around with her knitting needles sticking out. I was always untangling her when she'd go places. Those damned things were dangerous.

But she left her knitting behind, over on her side table. The needlepoint she was working on, the package is still left there next to it, unopéned. I'm guessing she took clothes and maybe a book or two?"

"I would go through her room again while we're waiting for the police, and see if anything's missing. But don't touch anything, or they're liable to accuse you of something. These good old boys are rather thorough, and they like to solve things quickly. Don't get in their way, Faith. Let them do their job. I doubt they have the resources to come in and look for finger-prints, but if this mystery goes on too long, they'll probably call in somebody else. Maybe the FBI."

"Already did that once before I called Mom, but I'll go do it again."

"Keep me updated, and if you need anything, or the police do, give them my card." He handed it to Faith.

She felt odd walking into Granny's room again, with morning sunlight pouring through her big picture window. The reason she'd moved across the hall to this unit was that it was brighter and more cheerful, she'd said. She and Grandpa Frank had occupied a one-bedroom suite across the hall with a nice view of the garden, but it was shaded, mostly because Frank had problems with his eyes and the sunlight bothered him. He was twenty years her senior and very fragile at the end, but he hung on until he was nearly a hundred before he passed over a year ago.

Faith did a careful perimeter search on all the surfaces without moving or touching anything, noting the pile of skeins as well as the large needles had fallen to the floor. She picked them up and lovingly set them back down on the nightstand beside the bed. Stroking the soft wool fibers, she pictured her grandmother knitting in her rocking chair, the click, click, click of the metal needles keeping time to the creak of the chair. She'd refused to wear glasses so started using the oversized needles the size of her index finger over the past year, due to her failing eyesight. Faith's mother had bought a special lamp with a magnifier in it for her needlepoint, which was also left behind.

Her favorite chair, something she'd had since she was a child, was in the corner, covered with a needlepoint tapestry her grandmother had made for her when she was ten. The colorful design had images of deep red roses and purple and pink peonies. An empty vase sat on the small two-person table right in front of the picture window between two folding chairs, one on either end where they used to sit and talk. Faith could almost hear her chatting right now, telling her how beautiful it was to sit there in the sun as she ate her breakfast or lunch, where she could look out into the colorful grounds beyond.

"You know, Sweetie, if I look carefully and squint my eyes, I can see the ocean!" she'd said one day, which surprised Faith. But if her grandmother thought she saw or heard the ocean, then she probably did.

Granny studied clouds and used to stay up late watching thunder and lightning from those very chairs. Her nurse told Faith that sometimes at two or three in the morning, during heavy thunder and lightning storms, her grandmother would stay up until dawn, transfixed by the power of the skies.

But now, Faith felt sad. Her grandmother's spirit had made this room magical, and now it was cold and dull. She missed her granny's smile. She missed the little girl look as her eyes got wide when Faith walked through the door, always happy to see her even if she was late, even if she had one of her own friend's children in tow or one of her nieces and nephews. She never minded that kids would jump on the bed or get into things in her bathroom. She was patient and loved watching children play. They made her laugh, she said.

While it was fun to visit her, after such visits when she had more than just her grandmother to look after, Faith was exhausted. So it didn't occur very often. She was hoping that someday she'd find a worthy man, get married, and perhaps start to have children of her own.

She really wanted Granny to see that happen.

Not that Faith was in a hurry. It was just one thing she wanted to see happen before her grandmother left this world. The two of them had never talked about it, but Faith believed her grandmother was counting the days expectantly.

"Ms. Goddard?" Faith heard behind her. Quickly turning, she saw a young, uniformed policewoman standing in the doorway with a clipboard. Faith extended her hand.

"I'm Jessica Lansing. I have a few questions I have to ask you, and I need to fill out this report so I can get it on the air if we put out an alert."

"No problem. I'm glad you're here. Do you want to sit down?" Faith offered her one of the two chairs.

As Jessica walked across the room, Faith noticed the young officer was extremely pregnant.

"Oh, thank you. Between packing thirty-five pounds on my hips and the extra probably forty pounds now for the new baby, my feet are a mess all the time, and I sit at every chance I'm invited. So thank you for that."

Her southern Tennessee drawl was soothing. Faith had spent her college years and part of her adulthood growing up in North Carolina, but she preferred the Tennessee drawl. It almost sounded like music to her ears. And of course, it always reminded her of her grandmother.

"When are you due?"

"I have three months left, although I think the baby is big, so maybe my dates are off."

"Before Christmas, then. That'll be fun for the family. Your parents must be ecstatic!"

She frowned. "Naw, it was always my mom and me, and she passed two summers ago now. But I got me a wonderful husband."

"I'm happy for you. I haven't found one of those yet," Faith said, suddenly feeling shy.

"Sweetheart, you're just a baby!"

They both laughed.

The policewoman shifted into work mode quickly. "When do you think this occurred?"

Faith shrugged her shoulders and started to answer but was cut off. "I know you don't know, and I will be asking the staff as well, but when did you find out about this and when were you told it occurred or when do you think it occurred? And did she say anything to you about going somewhere with somebody or by herself?"

"They called me at 8:30 this morning, and—"

"Who called you?" she asked.

"Mr. Jones, the male nurse that works mornings

here."

"Okay, and is he still here, or was he getting ready to leave his shift?"

"No, he's still here. I think they come on at 7:00, and they stay until early afternoon when the evening crew comes in. I think the person you really want to talk to is Sally, who is her attendant floor nurse. She's the one who really takes care of Grandma. She won't bathe or anything until Sally comes. Sally gets her cleaned up. It's kind of backwards, but if Sally worked mornings, then my grandma would take a bath or a shower in the morning. But since Sally works the afternoons, she does it in the afternoon. There's no way in the world she would let her have anybody but Sally touch her naked body."

The young policeman smiled sweetly. Adding more things on her clipboard, she asked another question. "So we think this occurred last night, or that's what they told you? And did they give you a time?"

"They said it was after everyone had gone to bed. I think they said it was something like eight o'clock. That's what the nurse told me."

"And she definitely left with someone?"

"Yes, they told me it was a man."

"Does your grandmother have men friends who come visit her?"

"No. There's nobody now. Her husband Frank died a year ago, and he was really her only friend, her best friend. They were married for, let's see, I think it was at least sixty, maybe sixty-two, years. Something like that."

"Wow. You don't hear about many of those these days, do you?" Officer Lansing said.

"Nope, you sure don't."

"Did anybody get a good look at this man, recognize him?"

"Again, that's a question for Sally."

"And you're sure she never told anybody she was expecting a visitor?"

"Not that I've been told. When we're done, I'm going to go over to her house just to see if perhaps she had some kind of a memory issue. I want to make sure everything's okay. It's vacant right now. Then I'm coming back to see Sally. My mother's orders. I think Sally is the one who holds the key to all of this."

"Sally comes on at 4:00 then, is that correct?"

"Yes, Ma'am."

"And you've not touched anything here?"

"I returned the knitting to the table. It fell on the floor."

They both looked over at her grandmother's made bed, her needlepoint pillows propped and designed the way they always were. The one that haunted Faith was the pillow made from a photograph of their favorite dog, Riley. Her grandmother had made the photo into a needlepoint canvas and had lovingly stitched his picture. Always standing guard, always watching over his mistress.

But today neither Frank nor Riley had protected her. She was just gone. Mysteriously gone without a trace. Faith broke into tears, so sorry that her sweet grandmother had come to such a dangerous place. She'd always thought her grandmother would go off into the clouds in a happily-ever-after scene like one of her romance novels, waiting to be reunited with Frank and Riley, all her sisters, cousins, and parents and grandparents. All the important people in her life.

This wasn't a happily ever after kind of day.

Chapter 2

Annie Carr

SWEET ROMANCE AUTHOR

F AITH DROVE DOWN the windy foothills of Beersheba Springs, Tennessee, toward the small town of Morganville. Her grandmother's house still stood in the woody acreage just south of the country road. She remembered as a child driving down the long driveway with her parents, passing the little sign that her grandfather, Frank, had made.

"Happy Acres."

The swing set was still in the front yard, although not in very good shape and listing to the right side. One of the canvas bucket swings on a long chain had come loose and was dragging on the ground. She stopped the car long enough to run over and re-hook the seat onto the grommet on the right side.

In a fit of whimsy, she sat in the seat, rocked back and forth on her heels, and looked at the woods, the sky, and the field in front of her. The garden that used to be her grandmother's vegetable garden was now overgrown with weeds. She was always battling the deer, and Frank had continually repaired a fence that got removed by tenacious predators. It was a constant fight, now given up, and left to Mother Nature herself.

It was quiet here. Faith's household growing up was noisy with all the kids, her parents very involved in the nursery business as well as school activities for her sisters and brother. Coming to Granny's house had been the respite she needed, and she'd come more than any of her siblings.

Always welcomed, Grandpa Frank would sometimes take her along on his house calls, being the only country doctor within twenty-five miles willing to do so. Oftentimes he took trades when farmers or retired homeowners living in ramshackle mobile homes couldn't pay their bill. Sometimes he'd come home with a chicken or a dozen eggs. One time, he came home with a little piglet Faith loved playing with, but her granny made him give it back.

They were grateful for what they received, and he enjoyed his work. She loved her grandfather dearly and found him to be the kindest gentleman she'd ever met.

Swinging lazily back and forth, she wondered how Granny liked living here as a young bride, raising her family, cherished and shadowed by the man she loved and who adored her in return. It was a true love story. One she never doubted. Of all the things in the world today, that was one thing she never would doubt.

When Grandpa Frank died, Faith thought she grieved more than anyone else in the family, except her grandmother. Granny stayed in bed for a whole week after the funeral, as if willing herself to die too. At least that's what Sally, her caretaker, said. She didn't want to talk about moving out of the one-bedroom apartment they had, she didn't want any of Frank's things touched, and she wouldn't even donate his clothes because they smelled like him.

The whole family was left just waiting until she was ready. And, in time, she was.

Faith wondered what it would be like to spend her whole life with someone and be loved and love that strongly. She was hoping. And though she was still in her mid-twenties, she knew these things would eventually happen in good time. And if it never did, she had her large close family. And family was the most important thing to her.

Her mother was always busy. An extremely brilliant and organized bookkeeper, she ran the nursery with an iron grip. All four of the kids had chores to do every day. A great big whiteboard was set up in the garage so they could check off when it was done, so she didn't have to yell across the field or go out on the tractor and find out if things were being handled to her satisfaction.

Faith thought she could have run a large corporation with her skills, although her interpersonal relationship skills were lacking a bit. Her dad, Noel, descended from a long line of landscapers and nursery men, patiently worked the land and the plants with his hands, never said much, and tended to the property as if it was his first love.

"It was delightful here," Faith said out loud.

She found memories bubbled up out of nowhere. There were initials carved into an oak tree at the other side of the creek. All kinds of special things she discovered over the years, like an old scooter, a wooden rocking horse, and an old watering can left to rust in the shed. Her grandparents' shed was her toy box. She had made castles and built houses out of excess lumber. She'd liked to speak to the handyman who came by and worked with her dad sometimes, who often came to give Grandpa Frank a hand. He planted a fruit orchard for them so Granny could make peach and cherry pies she used to win ribbons with at the County Fair.

Although her grandfather was good with his patients and healing people's psyches, he wasn't a handyman. Her grandmother was far better at fixing things, even mowers and trimmers and leaky windows, than her grandfather ever was.

Remembering what she was here for, Faith reluctantly got up out of the swing, made her way over to her open car door, and headed toward the house just a few feet up the driveway.

She was surprised to find the house unlocked. Her mother had told her they were in between tenants, but she suspected that local teenagers somehow broke in and made use of the house for a party pad from time to time. The family didn't come by to check very often because her mother lived an hour and a half away. Faith lived even farther. The rental agent they used was the town alcoholic, and she remembered her mother mentioning she couldn't speak to him after noon because he was drunk from then until he collapsed in bed after dark. That meant showings and repair scheduling and meeting with the owners or prospective tenants had to be done first thing in the morning.

The house had an unlived-in smell. When her grandmother lived here, it smelled of gingerbread and chocolate cookies. She was always baking bread or some of her fresh vegetable soups she was legendary for, which her grandfather sometimes brought to his patients. Several people in the area swore by her grandmother's chicken soup as being the best healing concoction ever invented.

"Hello? Anybody here?"

She heard some scurrying in the kitchen and knew it was probably an animal or bird of some kind. As she walked into the middle, she noticed a small mouse following the kickstand from underneath the sink, turning the corner, and exiting the back door through a hole chewed in the trim.

She made a mental note to let her mother know about this and perhaps to come back with some baited traps. And then, she thought to herself, since nobody was living here, it probably didn't matter. The little mouse probably wasn't hurting anything. Her grandmother had had problems with mice the whole time they lived here. So maybe they were just placeholders, waiting for somebody to come along and take it over.

The property had some history, although it was murky. Her grandfather received it as a result of a settlement of some kind. He'd owned a medical building downtown, and a gentleman he sold it to on a contract defaulted when the town rose up and said no to the thirteenth bar in the village. They had ten churches, but thirteen bars was just not going to cut it, not with a population of 1,200 at the time.

Now, the population was half that.

Most of the people who owned houses in the area used them as second homes, vacationing from Nashville or Lynchburg or one of the more affluent areas or renting it out for the vacation rental crowd that liked to go rustic in the woods. The house was made out of hand-hewn logs and was said to be a hundred years old.

Her grandfather had wanted to expand, but her grandmother was satisfied with the two bedrooms, so her mother and her two sisters had to share one of them while their brother slept out in the barn. That was the way things were in the 1960s and 1970s. They weren't hippies, but they didn't have a lot of money, and neither one of her grandparents wanted to move. So the family stayed.

Grandpa Frank had been happy there, and many years later, he very reluctantly moved into the care home in Beersheba Springs, but only after he cut his foot severely with a mower. The family got together and decided he needed more care and being so isolated from everyone was actually a risk to not only his health but her grandmother's. So they moved. And Beersheba Springs Rest Home was his final destination.

The kitchen walls were knotty pine. They had installed some big box store cabinets sometime during her mother's lifetime there, after some of the kids had moved out and they had funds to do so. Faith didn't remember any of that remodeling.

The house had everything in it except an extra bathroom. Her mother had stories about the fights that used to break out, especially between her and her brother, Lou.

Lou had joined the military in 1966 and was killed a year later in Vietnam. Of course, neither her granny nor her mother ever got over it.

The bathroom was musty, the floors very dirty, and the bedrooms needed the linens washed. However, the beds were well-made, and some of her grandmother's needlepoint pillows accented the rocking chairs in each room, the beds, and the large green velvet couch in front of the fireplace in the great room. As a child, Faith loved that couch, and Granny used to put her to bed in front of it with a big goose-down pillow and one of her colorful afghans. There wasn't anything in the world nicer than having a hot cup of cocoa and the loving hands of her grandmother tucking her in, her lips whispering to her just before she went to bed. She'd watch the fire until she fell asleep. Safe and secure, Faith thought she had the most idyllic life of any child on the planet.

Her phone rang, so she sat down at the pine drop leaf table to answer the call from her mother.

"Anything new?"

"No, Mom. I'm at the house, and it's going to need some work or at least a thorough cleaning. The mattresses definitely need to be replaced before renters move in."

"I don't mean the house, Faith. I mean Mother. Do you know where she is? Does it look like she's been there?"

"It doesn't look like anybody's been there for a long time, Mom. There's a mouse in the kitchen—at least one. The bathrooms, well, they're gross. The floors need to be cleaned and vacuumed. The paneling and furniture is all dry, the living room fireplace is overflowing with soot since nobody cleaned it after the last person was here. I haven't even looked at the refrigerator yet because I'm afraid what I'm going to see."

"Well, there's no power, so let's hope there's nothing there."

"Then I won't look, and there's not a chance in hell there's nothing there. There's bound to be some mold or something. But I'm just not of a mind to have that experience right now, you know?"

That got her mother laughing. It sounded good to hear it.

"Well, I think you should go back and see if you can talk to Sally. I tried putting in a call to her, but I told her you were going to meet her at the home and that the whole family had lots of questions. Once you finished with Sally, come on down here, and let's strategize what we're going to do. I think they've got all the bases covered there in Beersheba Springs. We need to contact a department up here maybe with a little more resources. It's just so old country up there. We really can't wait for them to get their act together."

"I agree with you, Mom. Okay. I'll head back. Anything new, I'll make sure to let you know. I'll try to get there tonight."

"Sounds good to me. You going to head back to Nashville or you going to stay with us a couple of days?"

"Well, I think I ought to stay until we make some plans about Granny. I'd like to find her or at least make sure somebody's on the case. Until that happens, I'm not going anywhere, Mom, and you shouldn't either."

"I agree with you a hundred percent, but Noel and I have a lot of work to do. It's spring season, so we're repotting and sending out orders. Timing couldn't be worse. I'm stuck here. I could also use a little bit of your help too. We've had to hire more staff."

"Well, let's look at the bright side, Mom. That means business is good."

"Yeah, too good."

Chapter 3

Annie Carr

FAITH GREETED THE chubby nurse who was her grandmother's favorite person at the home.

"Mm-mm, your grandmother sure has put us all in a tizzy. I don't know what the hell's gotten into her," Sally said shaking her head, her hands on her hips.

"Well, that's what I'm here to talk to you about."

"I gots to go down to the police department and talk to them. I don't like that. I wish they'd come to me. They ain't that busy, Faith. And I don't know what's the matter with everybody around here, but there's got to be a reason. Her mind was as clear as yours and mine right now. I do not understand for the life of me what could have happened. She didn't tell me at all about anybody coming to see her."

"Okay, so what do you think happened?" Faith asked her.

"God, I almost think there must have been some

Martians or something come down here in a spaceship and just take her off. I mean, she's such a sweet lady, your grandma. It's like somebody came to get her. Like maybe God called her. Maybe Jesus himself walked in and said, 'Sugar, you come and I want to spend eternity with you.' I mean that would seem a lot more likely than anything else I can think of. Peoples around here talking abduction, and well, you know what happens to old ladies when they get kidnapped. I don't mean to offend you, Faith, but you know full well that they get raped and left on the side of the road or cut up, you know. I mean they leave them somewhere. They don't kidnap them and store them somewhere. I mean those ladies that get taken, you know, they have no shelf life, Faith. You know what I mean?"

Despite the situation, Faith found herself giggling and worked to stifle it. It wasn't really funny, but she found the nurse's attitude refreshing, in a morbid kind of way. She shook her head.

"I know what you're thinking, Faith. You're thinking I'm the crazy one. You don't have to tell me. I knows it."

Faith knew she couldn't let her fall under this delusion. "Look, Sally," she reached out and touched the woman's forearm tenderly. "I know what you're saying. I agree with you. But this is the real world. And—"

Sally interrupted her. "Yes, it is the real world, God damn it. And I just think everybody ought to take a chill pill and put their heads together and talk about it. Somebody must have seen her leave."

Faith was thrilled to hear this. "Well, yes, somebody did see her with a bag, and she walked out with a man."

"I didn't see that, and I never said that. And I was here all night. Or at least until eight o'clock. There was no thunder or lightning last night, and so your granny was sound asleep in bed. There was no reason for her to be awake. She never wandered the halls once she did her pee and we cleaned her up. After I helped her shower and put on her fresh nighty, she was good to go. I put her socks on. She knew she wasn't supposed to get out of bed or she'd slip and fall with them socks. She would be lying on her back with her arms crossed in front of her, and if I went in and checked at midnight or even if I went in there at one or two in the morning, she'd be lying there in the same position. Used to scare me to death sometimes 'cause I'd walk in and wonder if she was dead. And then she'd breathe. That's just the way it was every single night. I don't understand what in the world is going on."

"Makes two of us. Just trying to figure it out, Sally. Fact from fiction."

"Do you have any enemies? I mean, anybody in your family heard or received any ransom notes or anything? Somebody out there looking for an insurance claim? You know, I think you all are really nice people. I have no reason to suspect any of you, but nobody here would do anything to her. She's a private patient, pays well, they tell me, and is no trouble. Absolutely no trouble at all."

Faith was alerted to the fact that Sally hadn't seen her herself. "So if you didn't see her leave with a man, who saw her?"

"I think it's Cory or Fred, maybe. The only people that really wander around here are the janitors, you know? The people that come in and clean up the floors if there's been an accident or taking stuff out. Sometimes they do little clean up things in the employee room. I don't know. They don't generally go into the rooms unless they're asked to, and I checked with the gals on duty. Nobody asked them to check on them. I mean, there were no incidents, okay? Nothing written in her chart. I just don't understand. Did you talk to the doc?"

She was referring to Dr. Craven.

"Yeah, I did. He doesn't understand either. He said that he'd seen her last week, not this week, but she was in perfect shape mentally. Nobody here seems to recall anything that went on that was unusual. It's just that somebody saw her walk out with a man."

"A man," Sally said, shaking her head. "I just can't see that. I got some ladies here that are horny as hell. They'd jump a broomstick and such. But not your granny. I mean, she never had any men friends come by, unless it was family members. Was this an old man or a young man?"

"I wasn't told."

"Boy, oh boy, isn't that a riddle then? I have no clue. I wish I did. You get them to check the hall tapes?"

"Do they have cameras? No one's explained that to me."

"You gotta know who to ask. I don't think they've fixed them." She grabbed Faith's arm and pulled her into the hallway. "We gots cameras up there," she pointed.

Faith was flabbergasted. "So who do I ask?"

"Security. But they don't work on Saturday or Sundays. You'll have to come back tomorrow or Tuesday."

Faith couldn't believe this was happening.

Sally had a sudden idea. "Maybe I should go through her papers and all her things." She stood up to start walking over to her grandmother's desk, and Faith stopped her.

"I was told not to mess with anything in the room in case they need it for evidence of some kind. So don't do that, Sally. I don't want to get you in trouble."

"Well, I don't want to get into trouble. I don't like the police around here. They make me nervous. And if I have to go down to the station, I'm going to call you first. And if I'm not back home or texting you to say that I'm done in like thirty minutes, I'm going to ask you to come down there and bail me out because I just don't trust those guys. Those good old boys, they can't tell a difference between a crime scene and a family gathering."

Faith understood exactly how she felt. It was why her mother wanted to get the Lynchburg police involved.

"Let me ask if we can go through her things. I'll do that first while I'm here. I'm going back up to Lynchburg tonight, so let's see if we can do a cursory look in her room, but I don't want to violate anything."

"Fine by me. I got some beds to change and some bed pans to sanitize. Lord, I got more work today, and it's stacking up. With all these damn questions, I even had the administrator call me into the office. Do you know how many times I've been in that office before?"

"I'm guessing none?" Faith figured she'd been wildly off because Sally drilled her a look like she had a huge purple wart on her forehead that blinked. "Sorry, just guessing," she shrugged.

"No, that's wrong. I've only been in there once before to ask for a raise, and that was the last time I ever did. The rest of the time all I do is dream about telling that guy off. Harrison is a nice man, overall, and he's pretty good looking too, but when I asked for a raise, he asked for a date in exchange. That was the last time I asked. Can you believe it? Now don't you go telling your mama because... Well, I don't know what she could do now. If your grandma's gone, she's gone, but I don't want any fight, and I need this job."

"My lips are sealed. And that doesn't surprise me either, Sally."

The charge nurse on duty advised Sally and Faith to not go through her grandmother's room. They were taping it off and asked the staff to stay out until further notice.

Faith tried to locate the two janitors Sally had mentioned and was told neither one of them came in, which she thought was rather unusual. So she reported it to the young policewoman who stopped by earlier.

"We'll check it out. I don't think I have all their information, but I'll get it from personnel."

"You bet. Thanks for being on this case. I'm going up to my mother's in Lynchburg. So if you need anything, you've got my cell phone. Let me know, and please, please let us know if there's anything at all that you find out. Anything, good or bad. We just want to know."

"No problem. I will surely do that. I've already gotten three frantic calls from your mother. Just between you and me, I think I'm going to call you back and not your mother. She sounds like she's wound a little too tight."

"That would be putting it mildly. Thanks, Jessica."

Faith thought about her mother the whole trip up to Lynchburg. It was near dusk when she pulled into the farm driveway, dodging several trucks piled with workers who were in the process of leaving the fields.

This time of year was always beautiful in the gardens. The cans of trees and plants all lined up in perfect rows, undisturbed by frantic activity as the trees would be shipped off to different places on order.

Her mother greeted her at the front porch.

"Are you hungry?" she asked.

"I could take a little something, come to think of it." Faith realized she hadn't eaten much of anything all day.

Her dad was talking to a couple of workers on the back porch and made his way in the kitchen, washing his hands. "How you doing, Sport? Any news about your granny?"

"Nope. I think Mom's right, though. I think you guys should use your contacts here to try to get somebody, maybe the FBI, involved. Although the policewoman I talked to seemed very nice, I don't have a really good feeling about that small community. You know they're not investigators. They're more like the cleanup crew and family mediators."

"Well, that's probably what they do. Probably most of what they do is arrest people for drunken disorderly, and I don't know," he dried his hands on the towel that Faith's mother gave him. "I just think there has to be an explanation somehow. Somebody knows something, and it just kind of fell through the cracks about telling us is all."

"That's what Sally said."

"Well, she sure loved Sally, so that holds a lot of weight with me then," said her mother. "Surely, she would have told her."

"Sally also told me there's a security camera there. But security won't be in until Monday, and she thinks it may be broken. So there is that."

"Oh, good Lord. This just doesn't get any better."

"Come here, Maggie," said her father, who drew her mother into his arms. "We're going to find her."

Her mother suddenly stiffened. "Oh, by the way,

your great-aunt Mavis is going to stop by and join us for a bite to eat. Gordon's bringing her over. She should be here any minute."

Her mother's Aunt Mavis was her grandmother's sister, five years older than she was, also living in an assisted facility but in the Lynchburg area. She was close to her family.

Faith helped her mother set the table for five and then poured water for everyone. They heard another car pull up the gravel driveway and honk just as it parked right next to Faith's car. Gordon, Mavis' elderly son, came around the car and helped his mother out. Although Mavis was twenty-five years older than her son, she was the spry one, and Gordon was the one who was hunched over. He also lived at the same assisted living home where Mavis was. He had never married.

"Come on, Mom, we're almost there. Watch your step. Watch your step. It's dark," he said to her.

Mavis' wiry frame steadfastly took the four steps of the porch, nearly dragging Gordon behind her. Her face showed a sneer, and she was about to scold Gordon about something when she saw Faith. That made her light up with a smile running from ear to ear, exposing her yellow teeth that protruded well in advance of her gums.

When Faith was little, she didn't like Aunt Mavis to get too close to her face because of the shape and condition of her teeth. It just didn't look natural, and she didn't like the way her breath smelled. But now, in later life, Faith understood that this simple woman was very hale and hearty and had a heart of gold.

"Faith, sweetheart, what a pleasant surprise."

Faith wondered to herself why Aunt Mavis would think it surprising she'd be involved since they were all dealing with the disappearance of her grandmother, Mavis' sister.

"Of course. We're going to find her. I know we'll find her, Aunt Mavis."

"I don't know. Sometimes that sister of mine, she had a mind of her own. You didn't know her when we were growing up."

"No. How could I? I'm almost sixty years younger than she is."

Gordon leaned over and whispered in Faith's ear, "Don't take no mind of Mom. You know she doesn't mean it."

"Mean what? Gordon, what the hell are you doing?"

"I'm helping you get inside, Mom. I'm starved, aren't you?"

"Oh, Lord. I can tell it's going to be a very difficult

ride home, isn't it?" Aunt Mavis said as she navigated her way through the front door, Gordon following behind her and tripping on the stoop at the end.

They were greeted with warm smiles and hugs. Mavis patted her dad's cheek and made small talk about the business. They were shown to their places, and Faith was given the seat right next to her aunt.

Faith's father began the blessing, as was their custom.

"Bless this food, Oh Lord, and please, please, bestow your tender loving care on our missing Rebecca. Keep her safe, wrap her in your arms, and bring her home to us. In Jesus' name, Amen."

Everyone at the table repeated the word, "Amen." The family sat together, discussing other family business and beginning to descend into some discussion of politics before Faith's mother called a halt to it.

"Wait a minute before we degenerate. I'm not going to talk about anything that's going to get any of us upset here. Our goal tonight is to strategize and talk about my mother. We want to find her, of course, and I need to ask all of you, have any of you been told anything by her? Did she call any of you or is there something that you might be able to shed light on this? We are all out of ideas. We've interviewed the staff, we've talked to the doctor, and we've questioned her nurse and several of the other people on staff there. Nobody has a clue what happened except for the one thing that one person said, that she left that home with a man and carried a suitcase. So far, it hasn't been corroborated."

"Actually, Mom, it was her knitting bag. Her big bag. Without her knitting or the needlepoint," Faith corrected.

The family whispered back and forth to each other, shaking their heads, hushed conversations to people at their sides. But Faith noted Aunt Mavis was quiet. The older woman wiped her mouth with her napkin and set it down, still clutching it in her left hand. She cleared her throat loudly. The room suddenly became quiet.

"I don't know if this is any kind of help or not. My sister and I weren't very close, but there are things from her past I didn't learn until years later. My mother, at one time, was worried about her running away. I don't remember why, but they had a big row. She told me to watch Rebecca and to inform her if I ever saw her getting ready to leave or if she ever confided in me about doing so. I did as I was told. And I didn't see anything. I couldn't get my sister to open up about what the big argument was with our mother. But about two weeks later, she took off."

Faith's mother was in shock. "Mavis! What are you

talking about?"

"She ran away from home. Just like my mother said she might. She didn't tell me; she didn't tell any of us where she was going. She ran away, and I never did hear what it was about. She ran away and came back about a week later."

"She came back home voluntarily?" Faith asked.

"Yup. She did. And we never talked about it ever again. She refused. But this running away thing? All I know is, she's done it before."

Chapter 4

Annie Carr

SWEET ROMANCE AUTHOR

I WAS AWAKENED by the sound of the waves crashing on the shore, pounding with the ocean's never-ending heartbeat. It called to me. My white nightie was no match for the wind as I opened the sliding glass door and felt the damp chill and saltwater scent blowing against me, fingering through my long white hair.

I wrapped up in my favorite shawl and stepped barefoot onto the patio, and in no time, I was walking across the sandy dunes to the still-warm loose sand leading toward the surf. I clutched the shawl to my chest, took in a big breath, and then let it all out.

I was free. I was home.

I stopped at the edge of the surf, listening to the foaming of the water seeping into the shore, tiny bubbles made by tinier creatures attempting to find new homes by burrowing into the sand. At night, the shore birds wouldn't bother them, not like the after-noons when they'd be the favored food to the winged creatures.

The moon was full with a fuzzy outline glowing in the night sky, hanging low in the fog hugging the shore.

A man's hands were on my shoulders, gently squeezing my flesh. I felt the heat of his body against my backside, the brush of his beard at the side of my cheek, as he planted a gentle kiss there.

"Do you see it, Jim? All the years we had? All those years and all the years to come still?"

"I do," he answered in that familiar raspy voice of his. "I lived them all. Every day, my love. You were with me every single day, through winter, spring, summer, and fall. I've been here waiting for you to return. Like you, I can see the future, Bex."

It had all started on a warm Florida beach in March. I wasn't looking for love, but everything was possible. This would be the time of my life. It would be something I'd mark as the most important milestone of my barely twenty years. Like a kite flowing across the blue sky, I didn't have a destination, except I wanted it all. I wanted the lush landscape of the beach scene, the youth springing out from all the shells, the sea grapes, the laughter, and free-flowing days in the sun with my friends.

It was 1964.

Yes, I was a child of the '60's. Whatever cares I had in the world were diminished by the beauty and freedom of just being in this place at this time in my life. About to embark on something extraordinary, something worthy of a memory that would haunt me in my sleep for the rest of my life.

Which was to say I was a good girl. My mother's child, her favorite one, I'd proffer. I had the kind of life my mother never had. She didn't complain about it, but she had been a preacher's daughter as well. While I helped at the church, my mom made sure I was free. The congregation did not judge me like they had her growing up. I was free to do whatever the world could extract from me. Away from my parent's prying eyes, I could take chances.

That summer, I would fall in love harder and with a fuller depth of feeling than I'd ever feel again—I'd throw caution to the wind in a reckless way no good girl would ever do. And, for the gift of all those warm, carefree spring days, I would pay dearly for the rest of my life.

Nothing thereafter would ever come close to the way he made me feel. To be in this kind of love— shameless, naked, dangerous love that tossed me down into the black pits of hell—I had partaken of the forbidden fruit and was left with no control over my trajectory.

Though it was the end of the fairy tale, I was lucky enough to find someone to save and preserve my miracle.

And so, I was redeemed. Just like her, I became my mother. I was devoted, dutiful, and cared for my husband and my growing family with no regrets, leaving behind my memories.

He loved me anyway. I'm talking about my husband of nearly sixty years, Frank. The kindest, most compassionate man, a true gentleman who knew he wasn't first on my dance card, but second, and occupied every line on it since. I was the goddess of his universe. He would heal and protect me to all eternity, and I loved him dearly for it.

He stayed by me in my ups and downs, my sadness and pain. He loved me harder than I deserved. Harder than I did myself. Sustaining me, loving me so much he let my magic linger and grow. He stood beside me, and together, we watched until *my* miracle became *our* miracle.

He was my first and only husband, even though my heart claimed he was second.

I WAS SUNNING myself on the beach when a football landed right on my belly. I'd been listening to my tiny turquoise transistor radio as the Beatles song "I Wanna Hold Your Hand" blared in my right ear. I'd been lip-synching along with the catchy tune. Children screamed as they splashed in the water. The four girls I traveled with down from Tennessee were building a big fort, a castle at the water's edge.

A shadow fell over me, and as I stared up into those deep blue eyes, I blushed.

"I'm sorry about that. Didn't mean to dive bomb you," he said.

I remembered the football that had rolled off my belly onto the towel beside me.

"I thought it was a rule: If it hits someone, they get to keep it."

"That's not *my* rule."

"But what if it's *mine*?" I asked him.

He bestowed upon me a bright smile and scratched his head. "My friends would call foul since the football doesn't belong to me but them. So I guess I'll have to owe you, because I have to bring that football back to the game or our side will have to forfeit."

"That sounds serious," I added, as I handed him back his leather pigskin.

"Oh, it is," he said as he accepted my gift. "I always

keep my promises, so we'll have to deal with the I.O.U. a little later."

I didn't want to appear too interested. The world of men was foreign to me. Most of the time, I had heart flutters from afar, not that I'd ever admit it to anyone. I slipped back on my black sunglasses and lay back down as if the whole interchange meant nothing to me.

"Suit yourself," I said, trying to be more casual than I felt.

He left, taking his shadow with him. My heart was flailing, trying desperately to catch up as he ran away.

Later on, my girlfriends befriended the football team, and I was formally introduced to James and his mates. We talked over hamburgers and chocolate sodas at the pier until dusk, when we all said our good-byes, but not without telling them what house we were renting on the beach. They revealed they had taken the house two doors down.

We agreed to meet up the next day, same time, same place.

I didn't sleep a wink all night long.

Chapter 5

Annie Carr

SWEET ROMANCE AUTHOR

W E PLAYED VOLLEYBALL so long the next day most of us were sporting a fairly severe sunburn by three o'clock in the afternoon. That's when we called it quits. All plans for going dancing in the evening were put on hold. Instead, the boys decided they'd treat us to good Italian food, homemade.

Louie, whose real name was Luigi, was from the Bronx, and his parents owned an Italian restaurant there, so they had an ace up their sleeve. We retired to our house to shower, take naps, and apply lots of soothing aloe vera gel.

"I knew I was going to pay for it. I just couldn't stop. It was so much fun," said Savannah.

"They are a nice bunch of guys. God, I hope they stay safe," Penny said with a frown.

I wondered what she meant.

"Becky, you know three of them are being drafted.

Jim and Pete are the only ones who weren't, and I think Jim's thinking about enlisting."

I hadn't been told that, although I did know they were going back home for work.

"Well, I guess we'll be praying for them, right?" I said.

Ashley angled her head and absent-mindedly stared off into the ceiling. "You know, Jim seems kind of sweet on you. He's not going back to California, he's staying here building houses. You could come down here and visit him anytime you like," she said, wiggling her eyebrows up and down.

I wouldn't know the first thing about how to handle this arrangement, and I let her know that.

"Oh, come on, Becky. I think he looks like the perfect type for you. He's sort of quiet like you are, and he's respectful. They all are respectful, aren't they?" Savannah was looking for approval, and the others nodded their heads in agreement.

"I'm not looking for a boyfriend. I got enough trouble just trying to figure out what school to go to and helping my parents with the church."

"Poor little preacher's daughter," Ashley teased.

"Stop it. That's not nice." I was getting prickly, or maybe it was the sunburn.

"You could get a job down here while you're trying

to decide," Savannah added.

"And then you could stay down here for a few weeks, see what happens. Nothing will happen if you don't take a little chance."

"Take a chance?" I barked back at them. "More like break my mother's heart. They need me at the church. Until I go away to college, that's where I belong."

"You could work at your grandpa's tree farm in Lynchburg."

"And do what? Repot trees? Straighten rows? Dig trenches with the workers? My parents are going to lose my sister, Mavis, when she gets married. I'm staying to help out until fall. I'm letting my apartment in Nashville go."

I'd been working in a vet hospital until I figured out if I wanted to go to veterinary school. I didn't like it, and my parents knew I was miserable there. So I was supposed to take Mavis' place and help out at the church until the fall semester. I would be heading up the summer Vacation Bible School program for them.

"You can't live your life for them, Becky."

"But my mom and dad are counting on it. You know ministers aren't paid much. Full time job, and the family comes second. I'll just be adding a little muscle, relieving them for those few months. It's out of the question to come down here. Least of all for a boy!"

They giggled, but Savannah came to my defense.

"She's trying to obey her parents. Don't take it too hard, Becky. We were just giving you some encouragement. Take a little risk. Do something for *you* for once."

"No, I've made up my mind and promised. I think Lou is going to help with the ranch after he graduates high school."

My brother loved working the ranch. With no other male heirs, since the death of Mom's brother, the family thought Lou would one day take over. But the farm was always struggling, just as the church was. Everyone in my family always did the right thing, even though it often meant there wasn't much opportunity for them to thrive. Not one of my family was good at business. We were the model citizens people looked up to and admired.

There was satisfaction in that, but it certainly wasn't a lot of fun.

"When do you start living for you, Becky?" Ashley asked me, her face completely devoid of expression.

It was a good question. And it was lovingly asked by friends I'd had since grade school. They were all going off to college, and I had no doubt they would make great choices and have wonderful careers.

I knew that if I got married and had a family, I'd be

expected to live close by to help take care of my parents, maybe work the ranch with Lou, but that would be years from now. I could see myself doing something else for a while before I'd knuckle down. But the decision had been made. Getting out would mean going off to college, and that wasn't going to happen until the fall. In the meantime, there was work to do.

The boys expected us over at six, so we bedded down for a short nap. When we got up, we showered again, got all that creepy gel off our bodies, then reapplied it, helped each other style our hair, put on our prettiest sundresses, and walked down the beach to their house.

The instant I walked inside, I was hit with heavenly scents of cooking foods: sausage, tomato, garlic, and all kinds of exotic spices. They had opera music blasting full tilt, Luigi occasionally singing along. He actually had a wonderful voice.

But the music was so loud you couldn't carry on a conversation anywhere in the little house. Jim greeted me warmly, but when I presented them a homemade pie I'd made the day before, I suddenly had four boyfriends, not the interest of one. If it wasn't for the fact my girlfriends protected me, that pie would've been the main course and we would've had our spaghetti and pizza for dessert.

We drank three or four bottles of wine during the three-course meal, which was very unlike me. At home, we didn't drink. Grandpa made his own wine, which was thick and full of sediment. But this was light and fruity and was delicious. I was a bit tipsy.

As the opera music was turned down and switched over to a jazz station, we started some serious conversations out on the patio watching the sunset.

"You know it's amazing how all these people come out here just to watch the sunset every night," said Penny. "It's like they're drawn to it. Like all these people in their houses are reeled out by some unseen hand, they come out on the beach and face the sunset like different colorful kites. They come out all at the same time every night. It's really strange. Kind of neat though, isn't it?"

"Yeah, it's a thing here. Definitely is." Jim looked over at me, smiling. "You want to take a walk? If you think the sunset is beautiful here, wait until you walk the beach with it."

I agreed. He held out his hand as we stepped up onto the dunes. I turned around when I heard giggling, which annoyed me. But I wanted to see what it would feel like to walk the beach and hold his hand, even though I had no idea what I was going to say.

We didn't speak until we got to the water's edge,

and then he directed me to turn right, toward Clearwater, as we headed north. The water came up around our toes and ankles, still warm. It wasn't going to be very cold tonight, which was one thing I liked way better about the east coast than the west coast.

"So how come you aren't going in the military like your buddies?" I asked.

"Well, they have low numbers and could be called up anytime. In fact, Kent was called up, so they signed up for special programs, Air Force and Navy, and he squeaked by. It's not very smart right now to get drafted, if you can help it. Things are bad over there from what I understand."

"What does that mean 'they have low numbers?'"

"Well, if you go to college, you have a deferment. I'm not in school right now, although I'm thinking about it. That might help me. But for the guys who are due to be drafted next, they kind of give you a heads-up when your number's low that you get called quicker. Instead of waiting to be stuck in the Army someplace, you can sign up for some kind of a training program you want to do. A lot of kids just rely on getting a good test score and getting into a specialized training that way, but it doesn't always work out. I have some construction experience, so if I had to go, I'd sign up for the SeaBees."

"The SeaBees, what are they?"

"It's the construction battalion. They build bridges, hospitals, landing strips, and things like that. They build roads and sometimes repair bridges or roads that were blown up. They kind of get ready for invasions, that's what they mostly do. I'm not sure what the projects are, but it's generally, I think, considered safer, although you still have to do some combat."

"Is there any way to get out of it?"

"You mean be a draft dodger?" He chuckled as if he thought my question ridiculous. "No, I've had a pretty good life. I owe it to my country. Not everybody feels that way, but hell, everybody I know is going in. I would sure feel bad if I didn't or I tried to evade it and some of my buddies died or paid the ultimate price. Just doesn't seem right, does it?"

"It doesn't seem right that people make up these stupid wars and then good guys like all of you have to go fight in them. That's what gets me."

He had that faraway look in his eyes as he smiled to the horizon. We could still see embers of the dying sun off in the distance. His face was glowing orange. He stopped. "I never really had a reason not to go. Maybe all that's about to change."

I thought I'd heard him incorrectly. My mouth got parched, my throat dried, and I tried to swallow but felt like I was swallowing my tongue. I wondered how in the world he would think that about me, and then I shrugged my shoulders and laughed. Of course, he wasn't thinking about me. He must be thinking about his buddies or about somebody else.

"What's so funny?"

"Well, I didn't think you had a girlfriend, so my apologies to her."

"What made you say that?"

"Your reason to not go. You decided to stay for her."

"Oh, I get it. Well, for your information, I don't have a girlfriend. But sometimes you meet someone and, all of a sudden, your perspective changes. Doesn't it, Becky?"

"I—I wouldn't know. I've only done the r—r—" I stopped.

I could tell by the way he looked at me that he was toying with my heartstrings. I liked it on one hand, but on the other, I knew I was treading on very dangerous ground.

I shook like a leaf in a hurricane, but I pretended to be brave and move forward. "I'm just here for a good time w-with my friends before they go off to school. I kind of wanted to spend some time with them before I refocus and go back to helping my parents at the church—my father is the pastor—my grandfather used to be as well, but had to take over the ranch—we had a sudden death in the family. I go sometimes helping my grandfather at the ranch—it's actually a tree farm."

I knew I was babbling on and probably boring him, so wrapped it up quickly.

"I-I need to finish some applications or decide what I want to do in college, what I want to do with the rest of my life. Not really sure what I'm doing. But—"

"Why don't you stay here? I'm going to be here. You'll at least have one friend in Florida."

I knew at that point I had to back up and reset things. I was suddenly nervous. This was going way too fast for me. And I was suspicious of his intentions, for the first time. I'd heard stories, of course. My older sister told me about boys she flirted with and dated, and then as soon as they got what they wanted, they dropped her like a hot potato. I wasn't interested in being that kind of a girl, yesterday's news, secondhand Becky. That wasn't slightly appealing to me, even if it was kind of risqué to think about it. But I knew deep down in my heart the quality of man I was looking for wouldn't do that to me. I didn't want to think of James that way, so I needed him to stop.

"You know, James, I think maybe you've got the wrong impression of me. I'm really not looking for that kind of adventure. I'm just looking for a few days of relaxation, a little bit of fun, and some things that I've never done before, like walk the beach with somebody like you, talk and laugh and cook, bodysurf, and play volleyball. Maybe go dancing."

"I'm on board with that. That sounds like good, clean fun to me."

He was so frustrating, how he kept the conversation veering back to "us" again. I was struggling like a bug in a spider web.

"We could have a lot of fun. Dancing, walking the beach every night, holding hands," he said as he held my hand up to show me.

I'd forgotten we were doing that. I immediately pulled away.

"James, we only met, what, yesterday? It's way too soon to be even considering this to be serious. I can't just move here."

"But I wish you'd reconsider."

I looked straight up into his eyes, without being able to admire the blue of them, and didn't see an ounce of regret there. He smiled, nodded, and stared down at his feet as he made squiggling circles with his big toe. Then he continued.

"I've been accused of making decisions too quickly. I'm a pretty good judge of character. I can tell a good person right away, and I think you are a good person, Becky. But I get it. I am not really interested in anything long term, either. I just thought maybe we could just let nature take its course, but you have to want to let it."

I stiffened a bit at the implied assumption that I might be interested in having some kind of a sexual relationship with him, and I had to correct that idea.

"I still don't think you understand me, James. That's not going to happen. I'm enjoying being around you and your group, but that's as far as it goes. Trust me when I say I'm not ready for anything else. And please don't lie to me and tell me I'm a good girl or I'm something special. I know better than to think that. I don't want to be led into something I don't want. So now that you know what I do and don't want, would you just leave me alone and respect what I said?"

"Absolutely. Becky, you have my word."

I was quiet the rest of the evening, and I didn't really care if others thought I was in a rotten mood. But I was very upset with the conversation, and I was really uneasy about the fact that I'd had to tell him these things. I wasn't afraid to show him I was way too young for this kind of random friendship that might lead to something else.

I knew a part of me was itching to do something

daring and exciting, but it was not where I was going to go. I was not interested in experimenting with my life or taking a detour, no matter how thrilling it might look on the outside.

I had always thought a long friendship, then a courtship, and then marriage would come before any kind of talk of a sexual relationship with somebody. That's the way I'd been raised. That's the way my mother had been raised, all the women in my family honestly. And as far as I knew, other than my aunt, everybody lived their lives the same way. Our church and our families were first always. Nobody would ever do anything that would shame the family name.

I asked to be excused as everyone was sitting around the fireplace out on the patio, telling them I wasn't feeling well. James offered to walk me down to the bungalow, and I asked him not to.

To the group, I tried to salvage what they might be thinking about me. "You know, when you first meet somebody, you want to keep a good impression. I might get sick on the way, and the last thing in the world I want to do is throw up where you can see me."

Everybody laughed. But James did not.

Savannah gave me the save. "It's the wine. Too much wine, Becky."

Once home, I sat in bed for several minutes before

I heard my other house companions come rolling in. I wondered if I had made a mistake. I felt sorry for the boys who were leaving to go to war. However, I was proud of the fact that I had stuck to my guns, that I had been my mother's daughter, that I had obeyed her and the family and put them first. I knew it was the right decision.

I just didn't know why it made me feel so terrible.

Chapter 6

Annie Carr

SWEET ROMANCE AUTHOR

WE DECIDED THAT today was a good day to go shopping, so we could stay out of the sun. We were on a quest to find large floppy hats that would cover most of our upper body area and sunglasses. Trying on hats and wandering around one of the large department stores, we were enacting scenes from *Breakfast at Tiffany's*.

We had lunch in the mall at a small cafe that also served cocktails. Putting on our big hats and dark glasses, we sat in the corner and people-watched all afternoon. We took a cab back toward the beach and spent the remaining hours of the afternoon combing through some of the tourist stores looking for knick-knacks and souvenirs. I bought an orange ceramic bank with the letters Florida printed across the top in green. I planned to use it for all my spare change until I left for college.

After the sun went down, we took a dip in the ocean thinking that the salt water would do our sunburns some good. We kept one eye peeled for the boys, but their house remained dark.

The next evening, we all went dancing at one of the Cuban clubs that had opened up recently near the pier. A little Latin combo was playing. The fish tacos and oysters came out on platters nonstop, and several of the guys ordered king crab, covering themselves in melted butter.

With all the dancing, drinking, and rich foods, I felt that I'd been more extravagant than I'd ever been in my life. It was as if I took my small-town experience from Tennessee and turned it into something huge, doing things I'd never done before, laughing and playing the part of someone else not at all like me. I even tried smoking cigarettes that night for the first time.

At one point during the evening, James asked me to dance. I felt more than a little tipsy, but I let him hold me. We swayed back and forth to the music. He smelled good. His body was tight, and as he twirled me around the floor, I loved that he was decisive, he was easy to take direction from, and he made me feel like we were the only two in the room. Even the sound of the music faded.

Every time I looked at him, he stared back at me. I got used to it, smiling, knowing he was watching my smile. I began to enjoy being the object of his intense gaze. My heart pounded as I turned and dipped, swung around, and then allowed myself to be held close against him. One by one, layers of my inhibitions began to shed, leaving me bare underneath, raw, excited, and electrified. I was falling loosely into the moment and into his arms.

And then on the way home, as we walked from the parking lot to our bungalow, he kissed me.

He didn't ask me first. He just pulled me to his chest and kissed me. I had absolutely no resistance to him, but he was still tender. I was suddenly unafraid. I knew I could stop him. But I didn't want to.

Savannah and Penny arrived home and interrupted our embrace. I took that as a sign I needed to slip back into the house. So we said goodnight, and I promised that I'd see him the next day. Exhausted, I fell into the bed and had colorful dreams, reliving the adventure.

All eight of us took a trip in two separate vehicles, driving across the state to the east coast of Florida. We went from Fort Pierce to St. Augustine. It was a beautiful drive. I don't think I ate anything but ice cream all day.

We took a set of rooms in the old town overlooking

the ocean. The hotel had seen better days. It was inexpensive, but the view was worth a million dollars. We stayed up talking, smoking cigarettes, and ordering room service. We drank tequila and told stories about our hometowns, our families, and our childhood. Then we delved into secrets, revealing things we'd never told anybody before.

Looking back on it later, I realized there really wasn't anything too awful about any of those stories, but it was fun and risqué.

Along the highway, heading back for our return the next day, we passed a group of young painters who were selling their sunset and palm tree paintings by the side of the road. James bought two of them, paying about ten bucks a piece for them. He offered me my choice, and I picked the one with the sunset and the palm tree.

We traveled back to the Gulf. I rode in the car with James, his arm around my shoulder as I snuggled against him in the backseat. We sang to the Beatles, Beach Boys, and Rolling Stones. The radio station played all kinds of hits, even occasionally Frank Sinatra, jazz, or show tunes.

Again, I was escorted to my front door, and this time, he asked if he could kiss me. I, of course, wasn't going to refuse him. I gave permission.

And that started the burning flame of desire I was never going to be able to put out. I was caught completely off guard. His hands roamed my body but not crossing the boundary of my clothing. I had to catch my breath. I was needy and desperate. I pulled away from our embrace just to look at his face and see in his eyes something I was hoping I would see. I didn't have words.

"I have to let you go, or I won't be able to tear myself away," he whispered.

I was confused, logic and desire playing with my emotions and not giving me any answers. "Yes, I think that's a good idea. I don't have the strength to send you away, James," I admitted.

"You're going to make me be the one to stop. Is that it?" he asked. "You gave me the hard job."

"I can't. I can't. You decide. You do what's right. I can't decide." I closed my eyes, hoping that he'd kiss me again. I was leaning into him.

He stiffened, stopping my forward trajectory. James gripped me by the shoulders, leaning in until his forehead pressed against mine. "I don't want to leave you. I'd like to stay with you tonight, and I think you'd like to as well, but I'm going to do the right thing."

"The right thing. What is the right thing, James?"

He released me. "That's why I have to leave,

Becky."

I watched him walk away, and I suddenly felt alone and so sorry I hadn't asked him to stay.

I wondered if I would regret that decision the rest of my life.

Chapter 7

Annie Carr

SWEET ROMANCE AUTHOR

F AITH HAD BEEN working in the greenhouse the last two days, transplanting little six-inch peat pots with seedlings of fruit trees into one-gallon plastic containers. This would be their home for the next year, and then they would move to three-gallon containers, trimmed and fertilized semi-annually, and be ready for sale the following year. It was mind-numbing work, so she listened with her EarPods to some of her favorite music. She switched over and listened to an audiobook as well.

The greenhouse smelled delightful. She'd always loved the scent of the damp, dark black soil in this ancient riverbed part of the country. The moist air soothed and caressed her skin. She much preferred doing this light work, almost like delicate needlepoint, as she'd pull the seedling out of the peat pot, examine the bottom tips of the roots, spread them and trim them as needed, and then place them in fresh, new cultivated soil. A little drink of water to top them off, and they were good to go.

The farm usually repotted everything this time of year, and Faith was already faster than two of the other helpers who had joined her in the greenhouse. But that came from years' experience, since she'd more or less been raised in and out of the nursery houses. She learned Spanish by playing with the farmworkers' kids and generally enjoyed the lifestyle of being outside, not being in an office.

She'd moved to Nashville after graduating from college with a degree in law. While she thought it would be exciting to work for an entertainment attorney, it turned out not to be quite what she'd hoped. She didn't want to be under her parents' thumb, but she had country roots, and she also needed to escape from the city. She wondered if there might be something in her future that would involve the nursery.

Her mother and father walked into the greenhouse, and the workers left.

Faith unplugged her EarPods, tucking them in her jacket pocket.

"You have some news?"

"I wish," her father said. "We're going to be heading to Nashville to meet with my friend who works out of the FBI field office there. We're hoping this will stir some action in Beersheba, since we're well past waiting time. We need action."

"I agree. I've got feelers all over the place too. Nothing has turned up. Absolutely nothing," Faith added.

"Your mother and I are also calling people that your grandmother knew, other staff members, former staff members, just trying to see if we can figure out anything at all about what was going on with her at the time she left. But at this point, we don't have any clearer idea what happened. And our only relief is the report from one person who said she looked like she was *willingly* going. But who knows what that means, Faith..."

Faith noted that both her mom and dad appeared to have aged ten years in the last three days since the news of Granny's disappearance.

"So then you'll need me to stay here. I've already called my boss and told him I wasn't sure when I was coming back. I explained what happened. He's agreed to help if you need it. It's not exactly his field of expertise, but it would be something you could use as a referral if you needed an attorney. And I understand the stress of not knowing what's happened to her. I'm pretty much running into that myself."

"We appreciate your sacrifice, Faith," her mother said.

"I actually have enjoyed doing this work, so I don't mind staying a few more days. It's not a permanent arrangement, though, and you're going to have to figure something out for that."

Her mother spoke next, beginning slow. "Your dad has hired a small crew. There's three of them who ran a wholesale nursery in the central California area. The nursery closed down and has fallen to subdivisions. You've probably read all the issues with water shortages and land with water rights being purchased by foreign investors or regulated by the government. They feel farming is going to be gone in California in the next ten years. The team saw our ads in the Southern Nursery magazine, looking for a project manager, and they're interested. They're going to be coming out tomorrow or the next day."

"Really? Wow. You move fast." Faith knew it was the smart thing to explore.

"They aren't definitely going to join us yet," her dad corrected, "but they want to take a look at our operation. We'd like you to try to keep them around until we get back. We scheduled this long before we knew about your grandma, and they just confirmed this morning. They're traveling a great distance, so we're taking it as a good sign they're interested. See if you can get them to wait for us." Her dad winked at her.

"I'll do my best. You know me."

A tiny twinge of disappointment entered her chest, nothing that a deep breath couldn't handle. Besides, Faith didn't have any money to invest and probably wouldn't for some time. What her parents needed was more immediate. And if her grandmother needed medical care of some kind, that would make the strain even more difficult.

Her mother softened her voice, low and sweet. "It's okay with us if you put them up in the house, but if you want to use the bunkhouse in the back, that's fine too. Whatever you think will work. They have good experience. All three of them graduated from the viticulture department at UC Davis, so they have excellent credentials. And they're looking forward to getting out of California, which is about right for us, right?"

Faith smiled at this. There were a lot of people from California coming to Tennessee, almost as many as were moving to Florida.

"Sounds good to me. So you think they'll come tomorrow?"

"Tomorrow or the next day. We've given them your phone number, so when they're a few hours out, they'll text you or give you a call to let you know. But yes. And I've also told them that we won't be here but that you were very familiar with the operation and grew up here, so they seem to be okay with that. I want you to put on your best sparkle. Be honest with them, but don't share anything financial—"

She interrupted her dad. "I don't know anything in particular financial, except I do know it's a struggle. What if they ask me that?"

"You can tell them that. You can tell them it's because it all falls on our shoulders. The workers are seasonal, and we need help if we're going to grow the business. That's what we'd like to do, our ultimate goal. We cut back a little bit this year so we could handle the business alone. But next year, we feel like we should expand."

"Sounds good. What about asking family members if they want to be a part of it?" Faith asked them.

"I think it's obvious to most of the family that this isn't a huge moneymaker. Nobody's come forward and expressed an interest. I doubt there is anybody who wants it. But maybe with someone from outside showing up, all of a sudden somebody in the family will get super interested. Things happen that way," her dad said, shrugging his shoulders.

Faith understood that about human nature as well.

She hugged her parents and wished them a safe journey. "Where are you staying?"

Her mother answered, "We're going to play it by ear. If we can find an Airbnb somewhere, that might work best, but we'll see. We can't meet with our friend until tomorrow morning, but we'll be there first thing. You take care, Sweetheart, and call us if you need anything."

"Well, make sure you give me the number of where you're staying, and I'd like to know you got there safe," Faith added.

Faith was finished with her table of re-pots so went outside to work in the vegetable garden. It was still very early in the season, and they could get a late frost sometimes even in April, so they didn't have any lettuce or tomatoes or summer plants planted. But they had lots of cabbage, broccoli, and kale. There were their personal fruit trees that needed pruning, and she quickly did that. She pulled out weeds that had managed to grow through the cold ground and made a note of some things she could pick up at the nursery to plant perhaps tomorrow before their guests arrived.

She went back to the farmhouse and thoroughly cleaned the kitchen, vacuumed the downstairs, wiped down the big family table with all the chairs around it, dusted and vacuumed the upstairs, changed all of the sheets on the beds, and started the laundry. It would take her until this time tomorrow to get through with everything and remake the beds, but she wanted to make sure that everything was clean and that no part of their living situation looked like it was in distress. Doing it, she thought of her grandmother. For years, Faith had watched her grandmother as she prepared to entertain guests at their little slice of Heaven.

She picked some blossoms from the garden, some early-flowering quince and an orange bush that seemed to bloom at all the wrong times of the year, giving off wonderful heady blooms that made her drunk with delight.

She also washed windows in all of the bedrooms and cleaned the two bathrooms for those bedrooms upstairs, as well as the master and the guestroom she was using, with its own private bath. She swept off the front porch and washed inside and outside the living room windows. She arranged the wicker furniture on the front porch and clipped back some dead or dying bottle brush blossoms and a few butterfly plants that had gone dormant. In the summertime, she used to have loads of monarchs flying through the yard and had planted special bushes that bloomed, attracting them. She also had several other varieties of butterflies that the neighbors got to also enjoy.

But the front porch was a little plain, so she made a note to pick up some more flowers, even if they'd freeze. At least they would be welcoming.

She took out some apples from the freezer and began to make an apple pie, a recipe that her grandmother had handed down to her, always a winner with guests of the ranch. She began making a pot of hardy beef stew and was planning on serving that with a green salad with lots of avocado.

As the pie was cooking, she checked the storage closet for a bottle or two of red wine she would offer them and put a bottle of white wine in the refrigerator. As soon as the pie was done, she checked her watch and had just enough time to run to town. She informed the ranch foreman where she was going and took her father's Jeep down to the hardware store where she could purchase some starts.

That gave her an idea, seeing all these colorful plants. She wondered if perhaps part of the greenhouse could be used for raising flowers to sell, maybe not on the wholesale market like they did the trees, but for local people who stopped by. They might even be able to sell eggs and chickens if her parents would go along with it. It was just something to attract attention to what they were doing, and although it wouldn't make a lot of money, it would help promote the ranch. It also would make for some colorful stories in some of the local magazines and papers. She'd heard of people doing ecotourism businesses where families could come and stay at a ranch and work for a week, to show their children what it's like to work in a nursery, which was very popular among young married couples with children.

The hardware store had a very short selection of colorful flowers, but she was able to get two flats of snapdragons, which could weather a late frost. She also grabbed marigolds and a flat of petunias, which she knew would die in frost. But they would look nice for about two weeks, and that was what she was aiming for.

She bought some minerals for their fruit trees and a new hand trowel, because the one her father used had gotten bent and was scarred from years of sorting through rocks in the soil. She also bought a new hoe that had a pointed face on it so she could weed and prepare the soil. She had all the manures she needed from the chickens, so she didn't need to buy bags of that.

Driving down the country road, the smell of the fresh produce in the back of her dad's Jeep and the way the landscape looked at this time of year, bare and just beginning to bud out, it was a happy place. It was similar to Granny's house except that it wasn't surrounded by the tall poplars and ash trees of her woods. But the nice rolling hills dotted with potted trees and rows of workers weeding and pruning and securing the irrigation looked very well organized and was a pleasant sight. She thought it was every bit as pretty as the lights at night in Nashville.

She brought the flowers out and set them on the porch, brought two buckets of chicken manure with her, and began to plant and arrange the colors. She added a dozen broccoli and a dozen kale plants to the vegetable garden but decided against planting more peas. She did manage to plant some sweet peas out by the pump, however, which would smell glorious in April and May.

It was almost dark when she finished her work, good work, good for the soil, good for her soul. She drank a small glass of wine as she sat on the porch and watched the sky darken. Deciding against dinner, she went upstairs, took a shower, put on her flannel nightie, and went to bed.

It was her bedroom growing up, and she remembered looking up at the beams in the ceiling as a child, imagining stories and faces of people appearing, as if it was a movie.

She was waiting for something. In the pit of her

stomach, she just knew that a great adventure was about to begin. She didn't know what she wanted, but she knew it was coming. It was as if the wind and the leaves and the birds and the flowers and the rows of trees and the big old creaky house told her so in so many whispers.

And this time, she was ready.

Chapter 8

SWEET ROMANCE AUTHOR

"**I**S THIS FAITH Goddard?" a raspy voice on the other end of the phone asked her.

"Yes! And you must be the guys from California?"

"Yes, ma'am. And we're about an hour and a half away. I believe it was your father who said to text or give you a call to let you know when we're in the area. I think we'll be there around noon. Would that work for you?"

"I'll be ready. Thanks for letting me know."

Faith reacted strongly to the casual California accent of the baritone voice on the other end of the line. It made her toes tingle. Was he the cavalry, the answer to her parent's prayers? Someone who could ride in and save the day?

As soon as the thought came, she chastised herself for being so ridiculous. But there was something about the catch in his voice, the way he spoke, something familiar yet excitingly different.

He did sound like a hero.

He was still waiting on the line, because she hadn't signed off. The pause was awkward. "I-I have plenty of things for lunch, so don't stop. We can have a little bite to eat, and then if you're up to it, I'll take you on a tour. I suppose you're going to want to turn in early. You've probably been driving all night."

She saw her reflection in her mother's china cabinet. She winced, one hand waving in the air, like a ten-year-old school girl with a crush. She didn't even know these guys. What was up with that?

Just as she began hitting her thigh with her fist, he chuckled.

"Well, the good thing about the three of us coming is that we get to take turns with the drive. But I don't sleep as well in the backseat of a truck, as I do in a regular bed so I will look forward to a nice shower. Yeah, I think I'll probably turn in early tonight. We probably all will."

"Well, there's not much to do around here, so you'll just be like all the rest of us locals then."

He sounded very nice, respectful, and young. Younger than she expected her father to have considered as a partner. She had all kinds of other questions about the two other people who were coming, but she was going to hold off on that. And she knew it wasn't exactly welcoming to pepper new visitors with information, especially before even meeting them.

"I'll see you around noon then. Drive safe. We don't have many speeders around here, but we do have a fair number of goats, dogs, and occasionally a milk cow that'll get out and wander the highways. You never know with these winding country roads. And then of course, there's always a school bus or two, just when you don't expect it."

"I consider myself duly warned, but I have to say, it sounds just like Madera, California, where I come from. And in my twenty-nine years, so far I've not managed to hit a single dog, goat, rabbit, or milk cow. And I've been driving since I was twelve, but don't tell your dad."

She loved his sense of humor. "Then you'll fit right in. See you soon."

They hung up, and Faith's heart thumped in her chest, nearly shaking the pine floors of her parents' home, rattling the windows. She was going to have to find some control, or she'd start making a fool of herself. She figured all this rose from the long years of working hard, going to law school, and never hanging around someone her age from the opposite sex.

She'd been working in the greenhouse in the morning and was just about to come inside to grab a bite to eat before the phone rang. She hadn't heard from her folks since last night when they texted her to say they'd arrived safely.

She dashed upstairs, stripped off her clothes, and took a shower. She worked extra hard to get the dirt out from around her fingernails then the brush to scrub her heels, in between her toes, and the lower parts of her legs and ankles where the mud and the dirt from the hoses would always collect.

With her hair freshly washed and a clean set of casual clothes, khakis and a white short-sleeved t-shirt with the Tennessee Tree Farm logo on the front of it, she felt remarkably better. She ground coffee, put water on, and also placed several bags of tea on a tray in case they were tea drinkers.

She caught herself mumbling to the table as she displayed the place settings. "I think half of California drinks tea, don't they? Oh, whatever. I don't have any decaf. They probably don't drink anything but decaf. Why didn't I think of that?"

And several choice self-reprimands flew out of her mouth before she could take them back. Shaking her head, she got out some lettuce and made a quick tuna fish salad with some tomatoes and her leftover balsamic vinaigrette. She added shredded cheese, thought better about it, and then decided she'd just make a new salad in case somebody was lactose intolerant.

"No telling what these Californians are like. They're weird. And they think Southerners are weird, too."

She finished setting the large family dining table for four. She filled up glasses with filtered water over ice cubes. In the middle of the table, she placed the pie that she'd made on a silver platter next to a pie server and a sharp knife. The salad was tossed and left in a large red bowl she'd inherited from her granny. It was her favorite bowl for making bread dough and swore by how it allowed the dough to rise.

Faith washed her hands, straightened her hair again, brushed her teeth for the third time today, took a long drink of water, and then tried to relax. She wondered if she should meditate or if she should just take a short nap, but she ruled both of those out. Nothing worse than coming up to the front porch and having your host be asleep or nodding off in the living room like an old lady.

The rumble of a truck engine caught her attention.

At last, she saw a dirty four-door pickup truck, sort of a deep army green color with off-road tires, the sides splattered with mud and debris from the trip, roaring down the driveway. It was impossible to see inside the cab since the windshield had been cleaned by running the wipers instead of actually wiping them clean at a gas station like she would've done.

They barreled down the gravel driveway a little too fast, so a small cloud of dust followed behind them. *God help them if an animal gets out in front of them.* That would tell anybody who was looking they were not locals, because everybody knew you didn't go that fast when you were driving up to somebody's farm. A polite visitor never wanted to create a dust storm that would cover porches and windows and everything in between. That was just bad manners.

Maybe he's just in a hurry to get here.

She stood on the porch and waved as a very tall drink of water type of man climbed out. He was lean but still muscular, wearing knee-high, dusty lace up well-worn boots. His jeans were a little on the tight side, especially snug in the middle and thighs and probably at his butt if he'd turn around.

It was Faith's thing. She always looked at a man's boots first. It told her a lot. Was he a flashy dresser? Trying to look taller than he was? Did he forget to clean them or just not care what anybody thought? She normally noticed if they wore knock-off expensive boots or if they were poorly made foreign imitations of something they thought looked "Southern." But his were just dusty, plain work boots, no splash, no lifts, no designs and certainly not anything one couldn't order online from a catalog.

She'd never greeted someone with dusty work boots that had never had a polish and certainly had never been cleaned. And he looked fine. Just fine.

Her eyes wandered up to his shoulders and upper torso, covered in a robin's egg blue linen work shirt. On his chest, he wore a silver medallion of some kind, and with the shirt opened one button more than normal, she got a good view of a very handsome and muscular body.

But that was before she saw his face. The blue of his eyes almost made her fall over. Her lungs were heavy, and it was hard to breathe. The golden strands of his hair, stiff as straw, glowed in the noonday sun.

While there were three of them standing there, he was by far the most handsome. The other two were dark-haired. One looked like he was Pacific Islander or perhaps South American, maybe from Mexico. He wore a handlebar mustache with huge brown eyes and shiny curly brown hair. The third one had straight brown hair, cut shorter than his buddies. He was the cowboy, she guessed, if there was one amongst the three. And after looking at his expensive boots, she was certain of it.

All three of them needed a shower and a shave, which she'd expected. She could guess they were tired from the drive. But she thanked the good Lord they didn't wear any ponytails or hippie stuff. No beads, no headbands. The driver did wear a silver wristband, and it looked like something he never took off, like his medallion. It wasn't jewelry, she thought. It was a statement.

And of course those blue eyes pierced right through her, all her second thoughts, and her mumblings, leaving her defenseless.

He came towards her. Now she wished she'd worn something a little nicer, not just her casual khakis, a t-shirt, and her inside-the-house work boots, which were a far cry from her outside-the-house work boots. Those boots were nearly as dusty and worn as the ones the driver wore. He ran up the steps so quickly she gasped.

Holding out his hand, he introduced himself. "Daniel Sorenson. You must be Faith, Noel Goddard's daughter, is that correct?"

All she could do was stand in front of him and stare into those eyes of his as if they were magnets. He started to move his hand away, and she discovered she'd been leaning toward him and hadn't offered her hand to his. It was awkward, but she placed her hand delicately inside his warm palm as he squeezed and shook for the both of them.

He's probably used to women falling all over themselves.

The touch of their hands, skin to skin, created an electric shock that zinged her all the way to her toes jammed in her work boots.

"Yes, I'm Faith Goddard. I'm the oldest of the Goddard clan. I'm here to show you around, and I've prepared a little bit of lunch if you guys are willing." She looked at the other two, and they eagerly nodded their heads.

There, that was easier than you thought.

She continued, "So I have a rule, and please don't be offended by this, but we take our shoes off at the door. I'm going to do that as well." She pointed to her own boots.

They spread out and sat on the porch, untying their shoes.

"Sure is pretty here," Daniel said as he removed his right boot first. "It was a gorgeous drive over. Glad we made it in the daytime."

The darker haired young man who appeared to be Spanish or South American or Pacific Islander introduced himself. "Rodrigo Morales," he said with a thick Latin accent.

"Where are you from?"

"I am a child of the world, Faith. But I tell people I come from California. My family is of Spanish ancestry, although we have lived in Mexico for many generations."

"Welcome to Tennessee, Rodrigo."

"And I'm Jason. I was his roommate in college and have been his best friend for more years than I care to remember." He pointed to Daniel. "We have trimmed a lot of vines together and made and drank a lot of wine too, some pretty good wine, if I do say so myself."

"Do you three have experience running a tree farm?"

"Well," Daniel said, "trees are trees. You need to give them a little nudge, some good soil—" He cupped his hands as if tenderly holding a root ball between them. "They need good fertilizer, some water, a little TLC. You talk to them. Sometimes you sing to them. Give them some vitamins now and then, rough up the soil around the roots, and tell them how pretty they are when they grow."

Faith was stunned with that analogy. She heard the other two chuckle.

Jason inserted the obvious. "He's just telling you the pickup line. He does it with all the pretty girls. But it works on trees too. He's a master gardener."

It works on women too…

"Well, I'm delighted to have you all here, and let's get started with our lunch. Then we can take a little tour. You want to get your bags afterwards? I guess I should have asked you that before you took your shoes off.

"Never mind. I'm hungry," Daniel answered.

"I'm starved," added Rodrigo.

"I need a drink of water," said Jason.

Faith kicked off her shoes and opened the door. The three entered their living room behind her.

She was self-conscious about the way they decorated the house. Since the family couldn't afford expensive furniture, most of the things they had in the house were hand-me-downs from second-hand stores and things that were painted several times, very colorful, some distressed looking. There were no curtains on the windows, because there was nobody to look inside. The rugs were old and threadbare here and there. Her grandfather's clock ticked in the background, and just as they were perusing the room, the chimes set off for twelve noon, with twelve healthy tones that echoed throughout the whole house.

"Well, this is it. Kind of simple. We're just country folk here. But we have a lot of room upstairs, or if you like, you can bed in the bunkhouse, which is actually quite adequate. The rooms are actually a little bigger.

From time to time, we have scout troops and church groups that come out and spend a weekend or a few days sometimes with their parents working on the farm with us, so that's more like dorm living out back. But my parents have granted you access to the house, so the house is yours if this is what you like."

"It's perfect, Faith. It's beautiful. Very welcoming," said Daniel. "Looks just like my grandmother's house in the valley. My grandparents were ranchers going back three generations too. They raised prunes and walnuts and for a while tried their luck at pigs. I hope you don't have pigs," he said with a big smile.

"Nope, we're not a pig family. Goats, we have goats, and they get into plenty of trouble. We have chickens and, of course, fresh eggs in the morning. We also have a couple of working dogs that belong to the crew. All our dogs are gone right now. My brother and two sisters are off at camp. So they'll be home in a day or two if you're still here. But come, let's have a seat, and we'll get ready to have some lunch. Please, take your places."

She motioned to the table, and everyone sat quietly while she brought out the tuna fish salad sandwiches. She let them know, if they didn't like it, she did have beef stew she had made the night before, a little bit of leftover cornbread, and the salad.

"Does anyone want a beer or wine? I can't say it's

expensive wine, probably not what you're used to, but we do have some. Anybody want something other than water?"

Everybody shook their heads no.

As they began to eat, devouring the sandwiches and crunching down on the salads, Rodrigo asked Faith how long her parents had been ranching.

"Well, we are third, almost fourth-generation. The ranch is something that has stayed in one side of the family or other. We all help out sometimes for harvest. Just recently with so many of the kids, my generation and older, moving away and traveling a lot more, there's less and less family to help us run it. So I think that's why my father thought, well, perhaps sharing the load with some new blood might work."

"How old is your dad? He sounds pretty young on the phone."

"He's sixty-two. He's a hardy sixty-two, a quiet man. He loves gardening, animals, and planting and gardening most of all."

"So was the ranch from his side or your mother's?" he asked.

"It's on my mom's side. My mom, my great grandmother. Not everybody in my immediate family ran it. It came to her from her grandparents, but my uncle, who was always supposed to be the one who would inherit the ranch, was killed. Luckily for her, she married a born rancher. My father."

"Well, that solves it, doesn't it? You can't make a farmer; a farmer has to be born that way. You got to love it so much that, even with all the hard work, back aches, and financial hardships, you still find it worth your soul. Unfortunate for us, we thought we were going to be able to stay on this ranch for our whole lives, but it wasn't to be. And the way things are in California, I don't think it ever will return to anything close to what it was. So it's time to look elsewhere. I've never lived in the South. In fact, I've never really known anybody from the South except kids we met at school, right?"

Daniel turned and looked at Jason and Rodrigo. The other two nodded. "But we've seen a lot of pictures, and it sure looks pretty out here. And I hear the people are real nice."

"We have our oddballs, just like you do."

"We're kind of done with California. So if this doesn't work here, we're going to keep moving until we find the right spot. We're on a quest."

Faith didn't want to tell him, of course, but that's exactly how she would describe her own journey as well. She was definitely on a quest. She didn't know what direction she was going or where the destination was, but she would know when she got there.

Chapter 9

Annie Carr

SWEET ROMANCE AUTHOR

F AITH TOOK THE three visitors around the nursery in their electric six-passenger golf cart. She drove them down the rows of trees in three-gallon pots, currently being segregated and pushed toward the delivery area by a handful of farmworkers. They were destined for shipment to nurseries all over the South. They even had several accounts in California, she told them.

She showed them the two greenhouses where they grew starts and did grafting and slip and cutting generation, as well as transplanting. She showed them the manure piles, brought in weekly from a local mushroom farm, the sandpit with both coarse and very fine grades of sand, and the fresh sawdust coming from a local lumber mill. There was also a pile of organic compost they had donated from a recycling center nearby, next to bags of soil amendments.

Then she drove around the perimeter fencing where roses marked the border, some of them quite old and planted back several generations. Those grew wild and didn't have to be pruned except once a decade.

She answered their questions about what varieties of fruit trees sold the best and where their biggest profit was, all the things she was authorized to tell them. She also showed them the bunkhouse and the small apartment where their caretaker used to live.

"You don't have one in there now?" Daniel asked.

"They last about a year, and then they move on to other things. My parents are a little bit strict on families and visitors, and in the past, we've had a little trouble with that. Drinking too. But by and large, when the good ones come along, we grab them for a while and learn from them and then they're always on to their better job. I think there's a lot of people who work here for the reference on their resume, to be honest with you."

"Well, I certainly can understand that. You guys have a wonderful reputation. Old family farm. There's just not a lot of those left."

"We have more of them, I think, in the South than you might in California. But land use policies are making it very difficult for this type of farming. We use a lot of water, and we need a lot of sunshine. We get a little bit of snow, a lot of rain, and more overcast skies. But as long as we get enough sun, we can grow things quite well and a little cheaper than some of the water scarce areas."

"It's absolutely beautiful, ma'am," said Jason. "I think you guys have a slice of Heaven here. It's sixty acres overall?"

"About that, yes. Not all of it is being used now. We cut back a little bit just so we could weather the storm. A lot of the landscaping and nursery businesses have had a hard time the last few years with the economy and the pandemic. But people are trying to bounce back, and we work with our buyers. We've extended credit probably better than anybody else out there. We know that if they don't get the trees they can't make the sales, so we try."

"You know that's one of the things about being a small family farm. You can do stuff like that. These big combines have to constantly be consistent with their pricing and customer base strategy. They have boards of directors to report to and people looking over their shoulders that will criticize. You guys can afford to give smaller nurseries a break, can't you?"

"Well, I think that's exactly who my mom and dad have tried to target. They can't compete with the big wholesale nurseries. But those big guys only deal with large store orders, not the mom-and-pop nurseries. I mean, I won't lie to you. I think my grandfather had big designs to have a huge warehouse for his nursery business and to ship exotic nut trees all over the world, but the fact of the matter is, you have to hire people to do things that don't even understand the nursery business. It's so dependent on so many things, and we understand farmers. We understand nurseries, and we understand sales, so we keep it manageable. All we have to do is just try to watch our profits and not lose too much doing something stupid, and we're good."

"What are you thinking about doing?" Jason asked.

"Well, a lot of people have suggested that we do Christmas trees, and we have a few over there." Faith pointed to a swale in the rolling hillside where several rows of small Christmas trees were growing.

"This isn't really that kind of weather, not quite cold enough, but you know, we can find varieties that would work. It's just that you have to cut them and store them, and the industries up in Oregon and Washington really kind of have a lock on that. What we do best is if someone wants to buy an ornamental tree that will be a Christmas tree in a pot for years on their porch, we sell those to nurseries, and those do okay. They are a little more labor intensive than some of our other pruning, and they have to be literally trimmed from stem to stern every year, not like some of our fruit trees."

"I see. Commitment. You have to have a higher level of commitment to grow those," said Daniel.

"If we wanted to focus on that a little more, that'd be something we could do. I also think we could do more with the animals. My parents don't want to get into that at all, but I do think we could have eggs and chickens and maybe even a small vegetable stand, just to sort of enhance our brand a bit? A lot of people know about Tennessee Tree Farm, but they don't know we have chickens and eggs. Usually, the truck drivers that come by to pick up our stuff, they know we got them, and they'll call ahead and order a few dozen."

"You have a small cottage industry already!" he answered.

"Yes, that's true. But I could see us having fifty or a hundred chickens. We could get a hundred dozen eggs every week, and with all the trimming and the pruning and leftover things that we can give them to eat, those chickens would be pretty healthy. A big vegetable garden throws off a lot of compost and gives the chickens a lot of healthy food to supplement the grains that they get too."

"Sounds like you've got a plan there, Faith. Are you going to be taking over someday?" Daniel asked.

"Absolutely not. Would you believe it, I'm a licensed attorney?"

That got a reaction out of all three of them.

"How the heck did you decide to become an attorney?" asked Rodrigo.

"I think, at the time, my father was having some trouble with a vendor, and he was also having a hard time finding a good attorney to help him. It made me so mad that I thought, okay, maybe if I get my license, I can help him. Of course, that's not really a viable job situation. The big money is in other types of attorney businesses, not collections and customer service. It was an ill-thought-out brain fart of mine. I regret it. But I know a lot about the law. I just don't care for being one of those guys who spends all their time in conflict."

Daniel gave her a high five. "Good on you. I hate attorneys. They're the ones who kicked us off the farm."

She showed the boys the duck pond they had created, which was a little devoid of animals since most of their ducks had flown off during the snow season. Then came the chicken coops, and she showed them the colored eggs they got, blue and green and purple. There was a small section where they had a heated incubator for raising baby chicks, and Faith explained to them that they only bred certain varieties, ones that were good egg producers.

"We want to have unusual colorful eggs but with chickens that are healthy and not getting sick all the time. Different areas use different varieties, but we like what we've started here, and we're sort of building our own flock as it were. The ones that don't do well or can't handle the cold or the rain, we wind up not breeding those. Most of those become tacos."

Everyone laughed.

On their way back to the house, Faith waved to several teams of workers who were stacking and organizing trees for a large pickup this afternoon. "My parents are going to be happy with this scene. Especially if the truck comes and picks them all up before they get home. That means money in the bank tomorrow."

"They're coming home today?"

"I haven't heard since last night, but that was the ETA. I wouldn't be surprised if they stay an extra day. My mom can always find things to do in Nashville."

Daniel spoke up. "I was there once right out of high school. Man, that was a crazy place. Lots of energy there."

The guys in the back seat seconded his call.

"It's a wild time down there. I love the music. I love especially Bluegrass. When it's a special occasion, we just hang out for an evening or go to an event. And there's always so much to do. I have an apartment in Nashville, and I think I still have a job, although I've missed a lot of days lately. Who knows, I might have a pink slip when I get back, and that would be okay."

"What do you mean?" he asked me.

"I need to find something else to do, and my family needs to find somebody who's really trained at this to help them, so I'm hoping this will work out for you guys. I will tell you this, my parents are two of the nicest people you'll ever run across. Honest, you never have to worry about them going back on their word about something. They're not motivated by profit but just to keep the farm going so that the next generation could perhaps make it more profitable. They're fine; they're comfortable. But they want to make sure they grow it for their heirs. And that's the sole reason."

Daniel looked across the seat at me dreamily. "Nah, that's not the only reason. They love the lifestyle, Faith. They probably couldn't see themselves doing anything else. I understand that. I'm the same way."

He was right. He did understand. He wasn't pretending. Daniel was not a fake. She could see that already.

Later on in the afternoon, Faith got a call from her parents letting her know they were going to stay over one more night. They asked how the boys were.

"They're really nice. I think they're genuinely interested in talking to you. I didn't give any particulars, except I showed them all the things I liked about the ranch. All the things I thought were good. You'll have to grill them about their experience. I know they enjoy the lifestyle. So it's not like they're moving here, so they could run off and go party somewhere else on the weekends. They're pretty down-to-earth guys. And they love working with nurseries and plants and growing things. I think you'll see a lot of good ideas coming from them. Probably things you haven't thought of."

"That's good, Faith. It sounds like you made an impression."

"I won't lie to you, Dad. Those guys are a little bit older than I am, but they're my kind of people. I mean, outside of ranching and doing this job, they'd be the sorts of people I'd hang around. I don't know anything about them personally or their families or if they have any backgrounds or anything. That's your job. But from what I can tell, they're pretty straight shooters, and they're genuinely interested in looking for new opportunity. A new adventure."

"Thanks, Faith."

"How about you? How did your meeting go?"

"Well, your mom and I are making some headway.

We had a long meeting with the FBI this morning. They are sending a couple of field agents, as we speak, to the rest home to interview everybody and to see if they can get their hands on the surveillance tape that is or is not there."

"Yeah, I thought that was really strange. You wonder why they would even have cameras if they don't use them."

"I'm not sure the management knows they're inoperable. And that's probably another issue altogether. The police are more thinking it's an inside job. Somebody that knows your grandma and she trusts them, like they were going to take her shopping or something. Have you heard about anybody like that other than Sally?"

"No, Sally's the one that comes to mind. In fact, I don't think anybody else has taken her shopping. But the whole place knows about her birthday party, Dad. Maybe it was somebody we don't pay any attention to that thought they would cash in on the opportunity. I just think she would tell us if she was safe, and that's the part that bothers me the most."

"That's what bothers the FBI the most too. We got to nail that. If it's a ransom, he says we would've heard by now. If she just wandered off with some other crazy person, then who knows? They could be out there in the homeless population or something, and that's something they're going to check on."

"Oh my God, you don't think she would do that, do you?"

"I'm sort of in Dr. Craven's camp. I think maybe she had a little mini stroke or something. And then got confused and did something. That seems more likely than anything else. Certainly more likely than what Sally told you."

"Oh, you heard about the Martians, did you?"

"Yeah, I know she didn't mean it, but that's what she told your mom too."

"Well, once I can, I'd like to do a thorough examination of the room. But I don't think they want me to touch anything yet. I really haven't been able to go through her things. You know there could be something hidden that we just don't know about that would explain it all. So when you're talking to the FBI, hopefully they'll get done with the processing, so we can actually go through and look for stuff that only we would know was new or different or didn't belong. I know there are clues in there somewhere. I just don't want to mess up the investigation in case it is a crime scene."

"How did I raise such a level-headed daughter?" he asked.

"I think it's because I got to spend a lot of time with Granny, Dad. Outside of you two, she's my most favorite person in the whole world. My life will not be the same without her. I just hope to God we get her back safe and sound."

She gave the visitors her parents' new ETA and, after dinner, took them out to the front porch where they lit up the fire pit. They sat in rocking chairs and wicker furniture that was always in need of repair and watched the sunset in the distance with her.

"This is nice. No bugs, crisp and clean."

"Oh, you should see it in the summertime. We got plenty of bugs here. It's not quite the tropics like down in Florida, but we get a fair share of bugs. It's also one of the reasons why this is an ideal location for the nursery. We don't have to spray, or we try not to anyway. It's just a little bit cold for what we're doing. Down south farther, things grow really quickly, but then you have to stay on top of the pests as well."

She wondered how all of them got interested in the farming business. One by one, they told their tale of either being raised on a farm or coming to visit farms. In Rodrigo's case, it was his first job doing landscaping for a large company who also did work pruning vineyards and maintaining large winery estates in Northern California. He wasn't as interested in the formal gardening part of his job as he was producing healthy vines, trees, and shrubs that enhanced the overall living area of wine country.

Daniel explained how his grandfather had a horse he used to ride in parades in California with some of his buddies, mostly combat vets. He'd never served in the military, but he respected his granddad a great deal and missed him.

Rodrigo and Jason excused themselves and went upstairs, which left Faith alone with Daniel. She'd felt rather relaxed the whole afternoon but now, being alone with him, experienced some of those heart flutters she had when he arrived today. It was hard to keep her eyes off him. And he seemed to be staring back at her every time she checked.

"You really thinking about leaving this place?" Daniel asked her.

"Well, it wasn't what I grew up thinking I would do. I wanted an adventure. That's the truth of it. Maybe I ought to hire on as a cook on a sailboat or something and travel. I like to travel. You can't go anywhere when you're tied down to a ranch like this."

"I understand."

"For instance, I've never been to California. I've never been to a winery outside of Tennessee."

"They have wineries in Tennessee?"

"Yes, some good ones. They have wineries all over now. You know they have wineries up in Canada too. It's not just certain areas, but I'd like to see what all the hype is about. Like why do people pay so much money to go to those places anyway? What is it about people that makes them do that and not be willing to do it here? I mean, this is totally beautiful. And there's other places I'd like to visit, like we all went with my grandmother to Florida one time, and she took us to the Gulf Coast. What a beautiful place that is. Now a winery or a nursery in that area? I think I'd give up everything in the world to have that. But this has been in my family, and this is what I'm supposed to do with my life, to help them as a thank you for what they've done for me. In the South, we're not like some of the people I've heard about out West who don't talk to their families, who don't even care what their kids do and leave them alone and let them go to the mall and spend money. You know we're different here. I like this lifestyle. I think it's healthier."

Daniel didn't say anything as he searched her face. Then he whispered as he leaned forward, his elbows on his knees, "What would it take to make you want to stay?"

Chapter 10

Annie Carr

SWEET ROMANCE AUTHOR

JAMES WAS WORKING today, having occasionally picked up jobs doing carpentry and miscellaneous construction work for a large contractor who was building and remodeling several of the bungalows along the beach. We went over to Pepper's burger joint on the pier, picked him up a hamburger and a milkshake, and decided to go over and visit him.

The boys knew where he was working.

The downstairs was fully encased in concrete blocks, with framing above for a peaked roof second-story that was more like an oversized attic. It was going to have a gorgeous view of the ocean from both the downstairs and the upstairs levels. James was working upstairs, framing the side walls and windows.

We waved to him from the beach. He was a sight— his tanned and bare upper torso made him look like a Greek god. His skin glinted in the sun; he'd oiled himself with sun protectant. But he had a tan line that showed when he bent over and his shorts drooped a bit to show some of his white flesh in peek-a-boo fashion, nearly exposing his butt region. The tool belt slung low along his waist and the fact that he didn't have very big hips also contributed to a possible shorts malfunction. He walked across the beams, baseball cap on backwards, balancing himself, his hammer clacketing behind him on the tool belt, until he jumped like a cat down to the stair landing and greeted us on the beach.

"Nice to see you guys. You had fun today?" he asked us, his gaze avoiding mine.

"Hell yeah, and we just brought you this." Troy handed him the hamburger and milkshake package. "We were going to bring you some French fries, but we ate them."

The four other boys shrugged their shoulders.

Savannah asked him, "How late do you work tonight?"

James gave her a very sexy look, in my opinion, and said, "Why, what did you have in mind?"

She danced around the sand and hid behind me, forcing me front and center opposite and close to James. Along the side of my face, she popped her head out and said, "Don't you think that's something you should ask Becky?"

"Absolutely, I'd love to ask Becky." He gave me a long, hungry gaze. "Becky," he said after he took a long drag on his straw. He licked his lips and looked at me with a sly smile on one side only, "Just what did you have in mind?"

One of the girls started fanning herself. Savannah let go of my shoulders, and as I turned to look at her, she rolled her eyes.

She was right. I had it bad. Really bad. This was not going to be good at all.

"I don't know. We just thought maybe you'd want to join us if we did something tonight is all. We can go dancing, go have pizza tonight, anything you like really," I said to him.

I hoped he didn't hear the creak in my voice, the flutter at the back of my tongue that made language near impossible.

He stepped closer to me, and my libido spiked. He was way closer than he had been before—at least in front of the others. "*Anything* I like?"

I decided not to step back, because I didn't want him to think that I was turning him down. I was only reiterating my boundaries. "That's what I said. Within reason, of course. And you know those reasons."

I didn't shrink from his gaze.

I watched his golden eyelashes flutter a bit as he

scanned my face, my arms and chest, and then looked back into my eyes. "I think I know you quite well, Becky. Can I ask a favor?"

"I suppose so."

"Can I change your name? You just don't seem like a Becky to me."

I was so disappointed. A name? He wanted to change my name? Whatever this was, I didn't like it.

"We call her Becca sometimes," Savannah said.

"I think I like Bex. Would you mind if I called you Bex? As in, I don't know—"

"Rhymes with sex? Is that what you're thinking James?" Luigi inserted.

"Well, that wasn't the reason, but as far as whether I've thought about it,—"

"Okay, this is not going to be anything we can do." Savannah was coming to my salvation. I was clueless and felt completely impotent. Frustrated.

I didn't think Bex was very sexy, and I told him so. I got the double-eyebrow lift of surprise out of him. "You want sexy? Rebecca. Is that better?"

"A little."

"Then Rebecca it shall be."

"So what time are you off?" I asked.

"I could leave at 5:00. Got to get home, take a shower, and change. Because I'm, you know, sweaty as hell," he said as he extended his arms out and showed his sweaty torso. "How about I meet you guys down at our house at, say, 5:30?"

"Are we driving or—?" Penny asked.

"Let's have seafood at the pier," he said to the group.

"Good idea!" one of the boys said.

I waved goodbye to him as James' contractor boss whistled and told him to get back to work. He held up the milkshake and the bag and yelled back to all of us, "Thank you!"

The four of us decided to get manicures and pedicures at a local salon, while the boys went to the bait shop and chartered a fishing boat to go fishing over the weekend. We sat side by side. I chose bright red for my toes and fingernails, but Savannah chose hot pink and the other two a more muted color, mauve pinks.

"You know, Becca, I really think he's nice. And I know he likes you a lot." Savannah sighed.

"I like him too. But, Savannah, we don't know each other very well. It's only been about four, maybe five days now. And how well can you know somebody in that period of time?"

Of course, I was lying to myself.

"Well, he respects you, right?"

"I haven't had much experience with guys at all. I

mean, not at all. And I just don't want to make a mistake, lead him on, or let him think he can try to get away with something, and then I have to be nasty toward him. I just don't want him to push me that far."

"Oh, I agree," said Ashley. "You don't want to date anybody that forces himself on you. But, oh my gosh... Bailey, my guy back home... Whenever I see him, I just can't keep my hands off him. We've probably gone a little further than you would be comfortable with, but he's a good guy, and we're just having fun. My mom got me on the pill, so I guess she kind of knows."

"I think most mothers do," said Savannah.

"With my mom, it's supposed to be a non-issue. I can't go too far. We're not supposed to do much until we get married in our family. And it's been that way for everybody in my family, as far as I know."

"Yeah, as far as you know. You know people do lie," Marley quipped.

Everybody giggled a bit. Even the manicurist laughed at that. "Oh, you should hear some of the lies I've heard. I met my husband while he was in the Philippines in the service. He told me all kinds of things, and when I came here, nothing was true. He even had a girlfriend here. Can you believe it?"

"But did you marry him?"

"Of course I married him. I didn't want to go

home. I miss my family, but I came over to be with him. He left his girlfriend, and we've been okay. I don't think he's perfect. I know he's a bad boy sometimes, but so am I!"

We all laughed at this, mostly laughing at her honesty and the fact that she wasn't telling herself a pack of lies.

"I could see writing and staying in touch. I think I'd like to do that," I added. "And if we could become friends over a long period of time, that would be wonderful. But I told him and I told all of you guys, I'm not interested in a romance. Especially a quicky romance."

"Well, you know what happens to guys when they have to go overseas, right? They get a little antsy, and some ladies think we should treat them a little special because maybe they won't come back," said Marley.

That certainly was the equation, and I'd heard it many times, spoken and muttered. I heard it on TV, even. It was not the ideal way to do things, but I did understand why they felt that way. They were going overseas, possibly never to return. The girl had to put out, it was said.

I still didn't subscribe to it.

"I think you can show respect for him without sleeping with him. There's no need to have to go that far. It doesn't matter to him if he's being sent off without a good sendoff. But if he's in a committed relationship in love with somebody, well then, I suppose it could be different, wouldn't it?" I said.

"I like your idea," said Savannah. "For a gal who has had no experience with men, you're handling him very well."

"Be careful of the handling part, okay, Sweetheart?" said the other manicurist.

Again, we burst out laughing. I could not believe we were actually having this conversation. And I knew it was something I would never be able to tell my mother about.

TRUE TO HIS word, we walked down to their house and found them all waiting outside by the fire pit. We strolled the short distance to the pier, and I couldn't get over how clean-cut and handsome he looked. He had shaved, he wore aftershave, and he'd put on a stark white shirt that really made his reddish-brown skin stand out. Of course, it also did a lot for his blue eyes as well.

The ten of us had not made reservations, but the restaurant owner gave us a large section in the corner with a great view of the beach on one side and the open Gulf on the other. We also could see the strings of houses being built and a couple of condominium complexes as well.

"You know, this whole area had several piers that have all gotten washed away with the hurricanes over the years. But there's an old wives' tale that says the Indians came here during hurricane season and were safe, and I think if you talk to people that live in Florida, they'll say that this particular area of the Gulf doesn't have the number of hurricanes and weather storms the rest does," James said.

"They have a town called Indian Rocks Beach," said Savannah. "I was listening to somebody telling a friend about it. They have magic rocks or something?"

"Yeah, they did a rain dance or something, and that seems to have held over the last hundred years. They've had I think only about 25% of the weather storms that everybody else has had," James answered.

"No wonder you love it," I said.

"What's not to love?"

We had chowder and French bread, drank too many margaritas, and also ordered crab and some grouper. James told me that grouper was a local fish, and I'd never heard of it before.

"They specialize here in grouper cheeks, fat fish cheeks is what they've got. It's a prehistoric fish. If you look, it's ugly as sin, but it tastes delicious."

I did sample some from his plate, and he was right.

I had literally stuffed myself with food, and the alcohol was beginning to get to me. The sun was setting, and within a half hour, it would be dark. One of the routines had been to go walk on the beach at sunset, so we all did that after our meal, needing a little bit of exercise, and I looked forward to working off some of the alcohol.

On our way back, James and I stayed behind at the shore while the rest of the group went up to the boys' house. I knew he wanted to talk to me about something, and I suspected it had to do with our very close encounter last night.

"Becca, Bex, Rebecca, I want to apologize about last night. I let it get too far. And I didn't mean to force you into something you weren't comfortable with."

"Thank you for that. I was confused."

He looked down at his toes as he made circles in the sand. "Yeah, I was too."

We stood next to each other, watching the glow on the horizon.

"Have you ever seen the green flash? Or is that just something that happens on the west coast?" I asked him.

"Yeah, I've heard people talk about it. I don't know if it happens here, but it does happen in California."

"You enjoy living in California?"

"It's fun. Lots of fun people. I personally think the beaches here are much nicer, and I like the weather here too, but California's fun, very exciting. There's lots of opportunity there. I don't know that I like the craziness of it, but for a young single guy like myself, it's kind of party city."

"Yes, I can see how that would be. You do Haight-Ashbury stuff, go up and look at the hippies at all?"

"You mean go to concerts and smoke joints and get stoned?"

"Something like that."

"Would it bother you if I said yes?"

"No, I don't think so."

"You liar. You're lying through your teeth right now, Becca. I know you wouldn't like it if I told you I ran around, went to parties, got stoned all the time, went to those big concerts, and dropped acid."

"Well, acid—"

He interrupted me by kissing my mouth very quickly. He was there before I could stop him. I didn't realize this was coming. I blushed and started to pull away but then melted into him again like I had done a couple of times before. His kiss was passionate but not demanding, not violent, very tender.

When he pulled away, he watched my face and

then moved his thumb over my lower lip. "I just couldn't help myself. I don't have a lot of days left here. We don't have a lot of days left. I just needed another kiss. I'm sorry if I threw you off balance."

I noticed he didn't say he was sorry he kissed me. He was just apologizing that he surprised me.

"I have no experience with men. So maybe this doesn't mean anything to you. But I think you're a really good kisser." I was proud of myself for my honesty and smiled.

He laughed, throwing his head back, and stepped away from me a bit with his hands in his pockets. "You mean compared to the other people you've kissed, right?"

"Well, I don't have that much—"

He kissed me again. "So compared to kissing your mom or your sisters or your dad?" He wrinkled his nose.

"Well, of course I don't kiss them like I kiss you. But you're the only person I've ever kissed before like this."

"Like how?"

"L—Like we just did."

"Show me. You kiss me, Becca. I want you to kiss me."

My heart was thumping, ready to come bursting

from my chest and splatter all over both of us. Of course my hands were sweaty, I had a hard time breathing, and I could tell that my skin was blotchy. I could feel the sweat develop underneath my armpits and behind my ears and at the nape of my neck, running all the way down to my butt crack. But I knew I had to try and show him the way I felt for him. So I did.

Very carefully, I stepped toward him, leaned into him while barely grazing the front of his shirt, and put my palms on his chest. With one hand drifting up the bottom of his neck to just beneath his ear, I leaned up into him and planted a kiss on his lips. He opened slightly, and I took a little opportunity there but not too much. I became timid and started to pull away, and then his arm wrapped around my waist, and he pulled me toward him.

We separated, and he placed his cheek next to mine, whispering, "That was the best kiss I have ever had. I want you to kiss me anytime you feel like it, Becca. Promise me that okay?"

Chapter 11

Annie Carr

SWEET ROMANCE AUTHOR

THE KISS HAD sparked something new for us. Neither one of us were in control anymore. We took turns saying no and then saying yes and then saying no again, only to take part in the joy of saying yes again. I think I said no so many times that saying yes was just part of the no. A gentle, sexy tug-of-war. I wanted to be reassured over and over again he'd practice restraint so I didn't have to. But there was a part of me that wished he wouldn't.

Each time I said no, he stopped. Each time I encouraged him, he went just a little bit further than he had been before. I can't say I wasn't thrilled, because I was totally invested in this relationship, wherever it took me.

"I know what you're struggling with, Rebecca. I know you want to be a virgin for your husband someday. And I care about you so much, I think I have to say I even love you so much, that I want that for you too. I don't want to damage your trust or cause you stress or regret. I'm never going to ask you to do something you don't want to do."

We were sitting on the beach. It was dark, but occasionally people would walk by. I felt very comfortable leaning against him, just as I felt comfortable with him taking his palm and letting it smooth over my back up and down my spine, eventually squeezing the back of my neck. Every place he touched me felt better. I'd begun to understand certain urges that I'd never felt before. I noticed some changes in my panties, the way my breath hitched, the way my breasts tingled, and how the very slight, almost accidental touch of his fingers anywhere on my body sent me straight to Heaven.

But I was torn between a place where I needed so much and the person I needed to be. I trusted him, and I trusted that he could take control and not cross that line. That part was a relief to me. It also meant I didn't have to worry about cutting him off harshly. We were beginning to build a trust between us I'd never had with anyone else, and certainly not with a man.

As he kissed me, I reached out to touch him as well. I caressed his face, traced his ears with my forefinger, pulled on his earlobes, and kissed his eyelids. I whispered things to him I don't even remember today except they were loving things. When he kissed me, I would tell him that it felt so nice. When he placed his hand underneath my blouse without going flesh on flesh and smoothed over the satin of my bra, I groaned into his ear. "Don't stop."

He could have done anything to me. I was that vulnerable and so willing to fall down that golden waterfall with him. I would have willingly lay back on the beach and spread my legs and given him everything I could. But he wanted me to come to him. He didn't want to be the aggressor. And it wasn't because he didn't want to; he just wanted to make sure it was something I wanted.

Every little touch was bringing me thrills I had no right to feel. Made me want to reciprocate. I knew that's what two people who loved each other did, but wasn't this play acting? Or the real thing? And how would I know for sure?

"Have you been in love before?" I asked him.

"Honestly, no, I don't think so. Don't get me wrong. I like girls."

"Have you been with a lot of girls?"

"Would that make a difference?"

I wasn't sure. "I don't know. It's none of my business, I guess."

"I think what you're asking is how do you compare to others I might have kissed."

"And done more?"

"What do you think?"

He brushed the hair from the back of my neck then placed a kiss there. My whole body tingled feeling his hot breath on my bare skin.

"I think you're experienced. You don't act nervous, like I do."

"Nervous about what? You don't have anything to fear from me."

"I am easily manipulated. Your experience gives you more confidence."

"But that's not a good enough reason to become experienced, Rebecca. You're doing all the right things. Who you are is more important than what you do."

"I'm afraid of making mistakes."

"Everyone does. You will too." He paused. "What is it you're really asking?"

"I guess I have this thing in my head that if I'm not experienced then I wouldn't be any fun. I wouldn't know how to kiss you properly. I wouldn't know what to do if—"

"But you kiss absolutely incredibly. Everything else—give it time. No rush on anything. When the right person comes along, you'll see."

"Have you gotten close to finding the right person?"

He thought about it, searching the dark horizon that was nearly invisible. "No. I can't say I have." He picked up my hand and kissed my palm. "But if I did, I think she'd look just like you." He kissed my palm again. "She'd taste like you, kiss like you. She'd make me feel proud to be in her company, lucky to be alive, and I'd never let her go."

We stood and walked a bit again down the beach, dipping our toes into the cool water. He turned and asked me, "You want to go see the house I'm helping to build?"

"Sure. The one you were at today? Are we allowed?"

"As long as no one else is there to say no."

"Okay, let's do it."

We got in his truck and traveled the short distance until the main road turned into a Beach Trail road, and then we found the sand driveway and the shell of the house in the distance. He turned off the motor, and we sat, looking at it.

After some time, he said, "Someday, I'm going to buy a house just like this one. I'm going to wake up every morning and see the beach, the sun and the white sand, and my life will be perfect."

"I love that vision. I know it will happen someday."

"Come on. Let's go inside."

We held hands as we navigated the construction debris. The moonlight gave us just enough vision keep us from stepping on rebar iron, buckets of nails, and butt ends of two-by-fours. We walked into the living room, and I saw for the first time that the second floor wouldn't be entirely covering the first—that the living room would be two stories and part of the upstairs would look down on the main living area below.

"I love this floorplan. Very open."

He agreed. "He's won some awards with his plans."

He took me to the sliding glass door opening to the patio. The surf looked silvery; the water swirled dark navy and light blue in the night. I went to open the door, and he stopped me.

"We just poured the slab today. Can't walk on it." He walked around me and put his arms around my waist, pulling me back into him. With his chin on my shoulder, he whispered his question, "Wouldn't it be wonderful to live here? Do you ever think you could live in a place like this, with someone like me?"

I let it sink in, afraid to spoil the moment. He let his question lie there in the ocean air, unanswered, and then I found my voice.

"What a life that would be, Jim. It would be incredible. Can you see the future, the years?"

"I can. I see it all, Rebecca."

He must have heard my sharp inhale, maybe the tension I felt all of a sudden, spoiling the moment I had hoped would last forever.

I started to explain but was being incoherent.

"Shhh, shhh. Nothing to fear. I was going a bit too fast for you. I apologize."

It was so unfair that there was this huge gap between us, mere strangers finding a connection to something greater than the both of us and having it cascade down around us almost without warning. I thought later if I'd had more time to get used to that something happening, maybe I could have navigated us to a neutral shore safely. If I hadn't been so young, I'd have known how to handle myself, but like a moth to the flame, I couldn't stay away, and that was making me nervous.

I knew there were boundaries I would not cross, and now I was entering into a conundrum. This was exactly the situation my aunt had told me about. Boys could be very sweet, very convincing, make you feel great. Then when the deed was done, you're forgotten. I just couldn't take the risk.

"I just don't have enough experience to know what I'm getting into here. I want to be a virgin for my husband. But God, if there ever was going to be an exception," I laughed to myself not because it was funny but because I really didn't know how to express it. I wanted to eat my words.

He turned me to face him in the moonlight. "Truth?"

I nodded my head and looked down.

"No, I mean truth, Rebecca. Look at me."

When I did, my eyes began to water. He saw, and then he scanned my mouth, my lips desiring his touch, hungry for the taste of him.

"I don't want to be your exception, Rebecca. I want to be your lover, full and honestly. Nothing held back, but only when you can. I want that for me, but I want it for you. I want to try to make it a forever kind of love, not just a one-night stand. Not a quick experiment in indulgence."

While I welcomed the sentiment, he wasn't doing anything to relieve my concern that I was falling into the point of no return. That I'd abandon my principles for something that was truly forbidden. I had dreamt about this, and those dreams felt real, but this was something completely off the charts. This was magic.

I was about to shatter the crystal ball.

"James, I can kiss you, I can touch you, I can be with you, I can talk to you, but as wonderful as it would be, I can't have sex with you. Don't ask that of me."

"Fair enough."

He turned away, letting me go.

I felt horrible. Though I was inexperienced, I knew exactly what he was talking about. I stared at his back, my heart aching for him to say something that would take the sting of what I'd said away. I stepped forward, leaning my head against his shoulder blades, feeling the thumping of his heart, the strength of his breathing in and out. Rolling my head, I kissed him there, right in the middle. I began to lift up his shirt, and I kissed his bare back, tasting him, inhaling his manly scent. I heard a guttural moan that came out of my own body as my knees shook and the juncture between my legs pulsed and got wet.

With my cheek pressed against his back, I whispered, "Show me, James. Show me how to love you."

Did that come from me?

He had the same reaction. He turned to face me, his hands on my chest, unbuttoning my shirt, his fingers pushing up under my bra to be the first man to touch my nipples, the first to kiss me there. He pulled me into him and against his package. I found my hands exploring the front of his pants, and then he stopped.

Pulling away, he backed up, still facing me.

"You would have let me, wouldn't you?"

"I wanted it. I still do, James."

"No. Not like this."

"Excuse me? Why the sudden—?"

"We're leaving tomorrow, and I don't think you know that."

"Tomorrow? No one said anything about—"

"This was their idea. Just wanted to go, thought it would be easier to leave. We're heading out early tomorrow morning. Troy and Kent got their orders. We found out this afternoon. That's why they came over to the house. They have to report on Saturday to Indoc. If they don't, they lose their spot. We're going back with them. I've also decided to join the Navy."

My head was spinning. "Wait a minute. Why? Why when you don't have to go?"

"I need to go, Rebecca. I can't avoid it when all my friends are risking their lives. I'd feel like a coward. This is too important."

"But your life is important too. Think about this, James. Don't do it."

"I have to."

My heart was shredded, completely shredded. And then anger began to boil up inside me. "All this talk, that was all B.S., and you know it. You're just like all the guys my sister told me about. Thank God we didn't—"

"Don't—"

He tried to hold me, but I wrenched myself loose.

"Don't touch me. I want to go back to the house. If you ever touch me again, I'll—"

"Rebecca, I love you. There. I've said it."

"Like that makes all this better? I want to leave."

"Let's not leave it this way. Please, hear me out."

"I've heard all I want to hear, James. God, I've been so stupid!"

"You're right. The timing sucks completely. I didn't think this through. I—"

"Shut up and take me home. Now!"

He took my hand and led me across the floor, through the construction debris and to his truck. I crossed my arms and stared angrily through the windshield as he ran in front and got in the driver's side.

How could I have been such a naïve idiot?

I was also embarrassed at what a fool I'd almost been. He'd set me up. Played me. Told me he loved me. It was clear he only loved himself.

I didn't say a word all the way back to the bungalow. Before he left, he shoved a piece of paper in my hand with his address and phone number on it. I was going to throw it away as soon as I got into the house.

Running to the front door, I didn't even look back as I slammed it behind me.

I heard the sound of his truck's engine fade away into the distance.

Savannah had waited up for me, but I really didn't want to talk to anyone. But she stopped me anyway.

"What did you do, Rebecca?"

"Nothing my mother would find fault with, except flirt with a con man. Did you guys know they are leaving tomorrow?"

"No, I had no clue."

"Good riddance."

Savannah eyed me cautiously. "So what's really going on? You've fallen for the guy, haven't you?"

"No, I haven't," I lied.

"The heart does what the heart does, Becky. We can't help it. Don't be mad or blame yourself. You did nothing wrong, or did you?"

"No. I'm still a virgin!" I yelled.

That did it. I'd woken up the house. Soon all four of them were sitting around me, asking questions. I told them about our friends leaving, but they didn't seem to care.

"Who needs them?" said Marley. "They were nice, but, really, I've got Bailey at home. We had a good time. That's all. It's done and over with. Now we can shop and do all sorts of fun stuff before we must get back."

Savannah said it best.

"Becky, honey, there are millions of nice guys out there. I mean it. Millions."

Chapter 12

Annie Carr

SWEET ROMANCE AUTHOR

THREE DAYS LATER, we were all back in Tennessee. My mother grilled me incessantly about my trip, hearing some strange stories from Savannah's mother, who was one of her best friends. Her friend was also a big gossip.

"Don't pay any attention to that. You know how Savannah exaggerates. Yes, we met some boys, but it was no big deal. They were partying before they had to go back to California. They're going over to Vietnam. They're heroes."

I saw she wasn't convinced.

"You know how guys are. We're fine. Really, Mother. Nothing for you to worry about."

She still didn't believe me.

In the weeks that followed, I threw myself into the Vacation Bible School curriculum and went up to Grandpa's farm to help out to earn some money for my fall plans, if I could concentrate on that, at least. I couldn't decide what to do anymore. Part of my future path had been erased and not replaced with an alternative. I knew I'd figure it out eventually. The church work was good for me, I told myself. But as time went on, it got no better.

I was still angry. I blamed James for completely cutting me down, ruining my confidence. I had trouble focusing on my normal life, my routine tasks, my planning, which always had been so easy. I'd feel those lips of his on my neck, his touch under my bra every time I put one on. It was so damned unfair.

Someone once told me blaming someone else for something I created was like ingesting rat poison and expecting the rat to die. I knew it was my fault. Me and my damned fantasy life. Thank God I stopped. What in the world was I thinking?

I'd been looking at the paper with his address and phone number on it in the middle drawer of my desk I shared with my sister, and then one day, it was gone. I asked her about it, and she cried and went straight to Mama. I received a scolding.

I never saw the piece of paper until years later, but it took me nearly two weeks to get over the fact that, even if I wanted to, I wouldn't be able to contact him.

Not that I had plans to.

And that made me mad too, that he was still coloring my dreams and daydreams, my thoughts in between thoughts, everything I did. When I baked pies, the pie crust felt like touching his skin. When I took a shower, I squeezed myself in places I shouldn't even think about. I looked at my face for evidence of blemishes and started wearing a little lipstick, which caused an argument with my mother, again. Was I thinking that because I'd had unclean thoughts that now I was some Jezebel?

And that made me mad most of all.

Two months to the day after our return, the phone rang, and I recognized his voice.

"I'm not interested—"

"Just hear me out, Rebecca. I want to apologize."

I heard clanging and activity in the background, even a siren, and I knew he was calling from a pay phone.

"I didn't handle that very well, and I'm so sorry that I hurt you. That was the furthest from my mind."

"Not convinced, James. You have no reason to call me."

"But I meant what I said. I love you, Rebecca. I've thought about it, and well, I can't stop thinking about you. Please, let me apologize."

"You already did."

"In person."

"No way."

"Give me a chance."

"The chance I almost gave you would have been a huge mistake. Huge mistake. James, just leave me alone."

"One chance. Let me buy you coffee. Just talk for a few minutes."

"We are talking."

And then suddenly I wondered something.

"Where are you?"

"Downtown Lynchburg. I came to see you. I'm headed back down to Florida for a week to earn some money, and then I'm leaving. So you'll be rid of me forever, maybe."

"Oh, stop that. That's an awful thought."

"Just hear me out. I need to make amends."

I knew the church had several twelve-step groups going on all week, and I'd heard the term making amends, so I took it seriously. But not too much.

But I was softening a bit.

"How are Troy and Kent?"

"Up in Great Lakes. Basic before they go off to medic school. Pete is going into the Air Force. Luigi is getting an exemption due to the family business. And get this, he met a girl after we got back, and they're getting married next month!"

It sounded oddly suspicious to me, but I kept it to myself. I didn't have to wait long.

"He knocked her up, but he really loves her," he whispered.

"I'll bet." I was disgusted with the situational ethics of Luigi's story.

"So I'm here. Can you come downtown and see me for just a few minutes?"

I knew the moment I caved. It was a memory of when he asked me to kiss him, and I willingly did. It felt so good—

"Where are you?"

"French Café on Broadway?"

I hesitated.

"Rebecca? Are you still there?"

"My parents are down at the church with my sister, and the other two are in school. I don't have a car, and I'm not walking that far."

"Okay, then I'll pick you up."

"That wouldn't do. Big scandal in my house if that were to happen."

"I don't think they'll ever know, will they? Just coffee."

I knew at the time it was going to be a mistake to give him the address. I didn't like the way he spontaneously decided things, but he was, in his heart, a good guy. He was the one who stopped, after all. I probably wasn't rational, but I decided it was safe for him to come to the house.

When I saw him out front, I realized my mistake. Of course he'd brought flowers—red roses, too. He was dressed nicely, not in cutoffs and tennis shoes or flip flops. I was glad I didn't have to explain who he was to anybody when he presented me with the two dozen roses and kissed me on the cheek.

"For you. Rebecca, my sincerest, most humble apology."

I couldn't help myself. I made the mistake of smiling at that. His blue eyes sent me places I had no right to be. All the familiar tingling was going on in all those places, and damn, he was so good looking when he was hungry. I was his prey. I should have seen it coming.

I brought the roses inside, placing them in one of my mother's crystal vases.

"Why don't I make coffee? Cheaper than the café."

"Sure."

"I made a pie too. You want some?"

"You drive a hard bargain. I'd love some."

He followed me to the dining room where I sat him down while I made the coffee. I sliced up a nice piece of apple pie and covered it with a dollop of vanilla ice cream and presented it to him. I sat at right angles to him and his coffee and pie and watched him eat and sighed.

That was another mistake.

He didn't seem so dangerous sitting there in my parent's dining room. Respectful and calm, he small talked until he began to grow quiet. I could tell he was thinking about something.

Was I worried? I should have been.

He leaned across the table and took my hand. "I've been reading about fate. Destiny. We fell in love, Rebecca, and that was a beautiful thing. I hold it as the most precious memory I have."

I winced. It was a little drippy, but he was trying.

"I think the two of us belong together, Rebecca. Do you—remember when I asked you if you could live in a house by the beach with someone like me? Remember what you said?"

I did remember that part, because I'd been hearing it replay over and over in my head for weeks now.

"I said I could."

"And could you still?"

I knew it was going to hurt. "Not now, I don't think."

"Why? Don't you feel what we have?"

I didn't want to feel it, but it was there anyway. I

looked away. He squeezed my hand.

"Come with me to Florida, just for a week."

"What? Oh, like this is a good idea. First, I tell you I wanted to save myself for my husband, and now you want to shack up with me for a week? No commitment? No ring? Why would I do that?"

"It would give me a chance to show you how much I love you. Just platonic. I won't touch you—well, I won't do anything you don't want me to do. After that week, if you never want to see me again, I'll understand. I'll fade into your memory—hopefully a happy memory."

"No."

He grinned at me. "Stubborn. I like that."

"Good, because that's all you're gonna get."

"Feisty. Aren't you curious?"

"About what?"

"What it would feel like to have a man worship you, someone who loves you? Maybe in time it will grow into something else. Something beautiful. A forever kind of love. I know it's rushed, and the timing on all this sucks to all heck, but I just wouldn't live with myself if I didn't try. If it was meant to be, let's give it a chance. Let me convince you of my love. You asked me once to go further, and I respected you. I stopped. I'll do the same thing again, if that's what you want. Let me show you that love I have inside, Rebecca."

I had not been expecting this at all.

"No."

"Okay," he regrouped, lacing his finger up and down the inside of my forearm. "We could write each other. I'm leaving soon for basic. I'm training for a new specialized unit that will be very dangerous. I would love for us to explore this connection between us before I go off to face that. Could you see yourself letting me try to make you fall in love with me? It's clear you don't want to, but what if I could convince you?"

"Sounds like you get all the goodies and I might lose my cherry. That hardly seems fair."

"No. That's not the plan. I just want to be with you, talk to you, walk the beach with you. I want to think about someone at home, happy and safe, when things are tough over there. Let me try to earn your love. I'm not talking about sex. I'm talking about love. Let me earn it."

In spite of myself, he was turning me on. I started to wonder if losing my virginity would actually be a good thing, something to "get over with" instead of cherishing and preserving it. I was thinking all kinds of foolish thoughts.

That silver-tongued rogue was doing a good job. I

could do worse. My parents would never give permission, so I told him so.

"Then come away with me. I promise I won't treat you with anything but respect. We'll take it slow. Open your heart to me, Rebecca. I don't want sex. I want magic. Pure magic."

"But I don't know you."

He moved closer to me, kissing the palm of my hand tenderly, touching my cheek, and slipping a strand of hair over my ear.

"You do. You know me very well. You know we belong together. You knew it just like I did, the first time we saw each other. That's the fate, the destiny part. It doesn't lie."

I was quiet, mostly to catch my breath and stop my shaking.

He continued. "And after seven days, you'll know me even better. Come on, Rebecca. Throw caution to the wind and come with me for just one teeny tiny week. I promise to transform your life, show you about love, real love. Take a chance on me. And when my hitch is up with the Navy, we'll get married. I'll buy a little house at the beach, just like we imagined."

I would think about this decision every single day of my life afterwards.

For whatever good it would do, I made him promise that if I wanted to return home at any time, he'd bring me back. I also made him promise that he wouldn't do anything to compromise me and my future. He agreed to both of those demands, profusely. I believed him.

I left my mother a note and told her I'd be back in a week. Something had come up. And I was with friends, safe, and not to worry. I told her I'd be home in seven days and asked her to trust me. I'd explain it all when I got back.

I knew she'd come completely unglued, but I chose my path, not hers, which in itself was a big change since most my growing up years I'd followed what my parents wanted. I'd now had a taste of something I'd possibly never get the chance to have again.

It was on that basis, that I wrote "Mother" on the envelope, sealed it, and left it on their bed.

Taking that chance, I packed up a small bag of clothes, washed the dishes, put away the coffee pot and cup he'd used, and drove down the driveway with him, sitting in the front seat of his truck.

It was the most foolish thing I've ever done before or since.

It changed my life forever.

Chapter 13

Annie Carr

SWEET ROMANCE AUTHOR

F AITH WAS UP early harvesting eggs for breakfast. The hens were restless, and she searched the gentle slope of their ranch for signs of a fox or some other predator. Although the coop was fully fenced and they were put away at night, some of their enemies would try to climb the fence. Although not able to get over, predators would scare them to fly out. That's where the carnage would begin.

One of her plans was to get the coop fully covered in hog wire, but that was going to cost more than they had to spend. Chickens, after all, her father had said, were a luxury, not a necessity.

Faith was going to try to change that opinion.

She dumped the scrap bucket at her feet and poured the other bucket full of laying feed into the covered feeder to keep it from spilling. She reset the automatic waterer, hosed off the bowl, and let it fill up with fresh water.

The chickens were happily eating and calmed down a little.

She used one of her buckets to get into the laying coop, finding two of her hens sitting on a clutch of eggs. Her big mother Cochins were great brooders and often the other hens would shoo them out, lay eggs in their box, and then let the Cochins sit on them.

And they were more than happy to do it.

Just like people. Some are brooders, some are adventure seekers, some have all the ideas, and some do all the work.

Behind her, she heard the gate creaking open.

Daniel was just entering the pen, closing it behind him. "Thought I'd give you a hand, if you need it."

He was wearing a light blue t-shirt with the farm logo from California. Faith couldn't keep her eyes off him.

He caught the message and stared down at his shirt. "Oh, this? Yeah, this is the farm we were at until last month. I have an extra if you want one."

"I'll trade you, like they do in soccer," she said.

"It's a deal."

"I've got eight eggs already. They've been busy," she said, showing him the red bucket.

He peered over the edge. "Blue, green, nice dark

brown one—"

"Those are the Marans. Cuckoo Marans are the only eggs James Bond ever ate. I'll bet you didn't know that? From Ian Fleming's books?"

"Dr. No. I've seen every one of them. You like the James Bond types?"

Her face flushed. "Not quite sure what type I'm into," she said, lowering her eyes.

They took the eggs into the kitchen where Faith began to make a cheesy scramble and some cornbread.

Daniel helped her unload the dishwasher and rinsed dishes she'd used to prepare. He wore a dishtowel over his shoulder, and she enjoyed the proximity to him. She was careful not to spill and not to bump into him, although when she did, that also was fun.

More than fun.

"What are your parents doing in Nashville?"

Faith wondered if she should tell him about Granny. Her dad didn't forbid her to.

"My grandmother, who lives in a rest home down in Beersheba, has gone missing. They're trying to get some help from an FBI field agent my father knows."

"When did this happen?"

"Four days ago."

"Did she wander off, or do you suspect foul play?"

"Someone came and got her. It was reported she

left with a man. That's what's got us all so stumped."

"A man? Whoa! How old is she?"

"Eighty, or will be in a week. We've been planning a huge family party for her for weeks. She was looking forward to it. She's never done anything like this before, and she's fully cognizant—her brain is functioning on all cylinders."

"Did she leave a message with anyone? Who's close to her?"

"I am the closest now of the family, mostly because I have more time than anyone else does. She didn't say anything to me. I have no clue what she's up to, and it's not like her not to check in. And yet, she appears to have gone willingly. Just slipped out the door at night with a bag packed. It was so low-key no one took notice. Everyone thought someone else knew about it."

"Your parents must be frantic with worry."

"We all are."

He leaned toward her and whispered, "She has a secret lover, I'll bet."

He said what she'd been thinking for a couple of days but never wanted to tell anyone or say it out loud. She scanned his handsome face, the blue eyes giving her comfort, smiling lines at the edges. "At eighty? She's never talked about anyone from her past. She was married to my grandfather for nearly sixty years."

"And your grandfather didn't come back from the grave, right?"

Faith burst out laughing. "Hardly."

"There has to be a logical explanation."

"Well, it's gone on too long. We're afraid the investigation hasn't reached a critical enough phase. If she's out there in the elements, she could be dead by now. We're rural here. Don't quite have the resources. I wish they hadn't waited so long. And then there's part of me that thinks she just fell prey to some pervert or something. You never think anything like this could happen to someone you love, but it does. Real life isn't kind."

"I'm so sorry. And our timing now kind of sucks."

"No, Dad and Mom are very much looking forward to your visit." They heard sounds indicating the other two guests were up.

"Daniel, help me get these on the table while I take the cornbread out."

She'd forgotten to cook the bacon she'd planned, but the eggs and cornbread were a big hit. They had just finished their late breakfast when she heard her parents drive down the driveway.

Faith introduced the visitors. Her father welcomed them while her mother retreated to the bedroom. She knew something was wrong, excusing herself to follow her upstairs.

"Mom, is everything all right?"

Her mother was sitting on the bed, dabbing her eyes with a tissue. She sighed, looked up at Faith, her eyes rheumy and red. But she didn't say a word.

Faith sat next to her.

"Hey. What is it?"

"Noel's friend did some digging. Back before I was born, before she married your grandfather, there was a file under her name. My granddad had started to file a complaint against someone who had—who—"

"What, what is it?"

"Your granny may have been molested by someone a long time ago. It never went to court because it was never formally placed, but the police notes were there staring us in the face. Noel's friend thinks your great-grandpa did it so he wouldn't embroil my mom in a scandal of some kind. He was trying to shield her. The last note in the file was 'Refuses to Prosecute' and something about Mom being an uncooperative victim."

Faith immediately thought about Daniel's comment. Maybe he'd been right.

"You think—?"

"We don't know, Faith. But they are looking for him, the man, I mean."

"Did Grandpa Frank know?" she asked her mother.

"I don't think so. It was before his time. But it breaks my heart to now know that your grandmother had a very dark secret. I wish she'd confided in me before it was too late. Now? God knows what's going to happen. He's trying to build a case to issue an arrest warrant. But no one knows where to look for him or for her."

Chapter 14

Annie Carr

SWEET ROMANCE AUTHOR

F AITH KNEW WHAT she should do. She had to get into her grandmother's room at the home, confident that, if she did, she'd find some clue, something that gave her an idea what happened to her grandmother and where she had gone.

She discussed doing this with her parents. Daniel overheard and asked, once they gave their permission, to go along with her.

"Faith, now, don't you go barging in there ruining their investigation," her father cautioned. "If they're not done, you could be prosecuted for interfering with a crime scene."

"Remember who you're talking to, Dad. I am an attorney."

"Nonetheless, you go off half-cocked sometimes. We all do dumb things from time to time when we feel moved, and you don't want to make everything worse.

You might disturb his fingerprints, something that would be crucial to finding him and thereby finding her."

"But you're not even sure he's responsible for this, right?"

Her father faltered. Her mother inserted, "Based on his years of experience, Faith, honey, the agent thinks this is the best lead we have so far. He called it his hunch, and he told us, with missing persons, hunches were very important to follow. All the leads had to be followed up."

"What would be his motive? To get even? For what?" Daniel asked.

"Son, people do all kinds of whacko things all the time. You know that. You lived in California for Chrissake!"

"Noel—" Her mother reached over and grabbed his hand. "Use your head. These boys are out here to look at the farm. Let's not blow everything up. One crisis at a time, please. Will you try to keep your composure?"

"Unfortunately, I think there are very evil men out there. Maybe you can live under the naïve theory that people are basically good. I wish like Hell it was true. The plain truth is there are horrible people out there doing horrible things. Maybe this guy was fixated on her, stalked her until she was vulnerable. It was at nighttime. She was in her nightie!"

Faith rolled her eyes at Daniel. Her grandmother being in her nightgown in front of a strange man was the least of their concerns. The big problem was finding her before she was gone forever. Her dad was a typical protector, but right now, it wasn't helping.

"Mr. Goddard," Daniel began, "I really want to help. Let me take Faith down there to have a look around. I promise I'll stay right by her side. I won't let any harm come to her, and I'll make sure we work around the authorities too. It sounds like Faith and your mother—"

"Mother-in-law," he corrected.

Mrs. Goddard started to cry.

"Okay, mother-in-law then. They have a special bond, from what Faith's been telling me. You don't want her driving when she's upset like this. I'll do that. I'll make sure she gets down there safely and gets back with whatever we can find. But let your daughter search through her grandmother's things. Maybe there is something hidden there only she will recognize."

Faith added, "In the meantime, you two will be here to catch any follow-up calls. And if we find anything, we'll call you right away so you are kept in the loop, Dad. Please, I just can't sit around and do nothing. I feel so helpless."

Faith's mother checked her watch. "It'll be dark when you get down there. Maybe you should go tomorrow morning."

"No. I don't want to waste any more time."

"But where will you stay?" her father asked.

"I'll stay at Granny's house. I'll need to borrow some sleeping bags and a couple of pillows, since the mattresses are probably full of dust and pests."

"I'll go get my fishing pack. That has everything in there you need, and I just washed everything last time out. You'll be warm. There's a little cook stove and some freeze-dried food packets, if you want them."

DANIEL BARRELED DOWN the driveway after saying good-bye to his two fellow travelers, who had also offered to go, but Faith's father wouldn't allow it. She asked him to slow down.

"Just trying to do my job, Faith."

"There's this little thing, when you live in the country. Only city slickers drive like a bat out of hell on someone's gravel driveway, unless they are truly angry or something. Don't you watch how fast you drive through the vineyards back there in California? We don't like to get our front porches and gardens sprayed with dust."

"O-kay." he said, showing a bit of attitude. He

slowed down to a crawl, checking the rear-view mirror to satisfy himself there was no dust being kicked up.

"Sorry," she answered.

It wasn't until after they got onto the highway that they talked. Daniel began.

"You know, I didn't have to do this. I didn't come all this distance to go camping in Tennessee in March. I came out here to look at a nursery. What I found was a whole lot more family drama than I'd bargained for. So excuse me if I look too 'city' for you, but I'm actually a farm boy, and when you call me a 'city slicker' that just hurts my feelings."

Faith turned and snatched a look at his wincing face. He was mad.

"It's not your granny who's missing."

"No, thankfully, it's not. My gramma is dead, Faith. Thank you very much."

She felt horrible now. She whispered, "I didn't know."

He glanced over at her. "Of course you didn't know. How the hell would you know that? Just like how was I to know that your grandmother ran off with her old lover—"

"Wait a minute, Daniel. You have no right to say that. He could be a stalker, a bad man, coming back after years of, of—I don't know."

"Two people. In their eighties. What do you think this is about?"

"Well, it's not about sex, that's for damned sure," she answered. Now she was building into a full-blown explosion starting from her gut and sucking all the air from the cab of the truck.

"I'll have you know my family has sex way until their nineties."

She sat there, blinking, not sure how she should respond to that. She'd never heard that before, but then, she'd never thought about it, either.

"I guess you guys are a little repressed here in Tennessee."

"Stop it. Stop the truck. You're taking me back."

"The hell I am. We're going down to wherever Bathsheba—"

"Beersheba Springs," she corrected.

"Not like in the Bible?"

"Of course not. This is Tennessee." She was into a full-blown pout, her arms crossed, even her legs were crossed, cramped under the weight of the shoulder harness seatbelt.

Daniel laughed at that. "Oh, now I get it. Of course. What was I thinking, anyway?"

He turned to look at her, and she met his gaze. Suddenly, they both were laughing so hard she almost peed her pants.

When they got to the rest home, Sally was waiting for them. Her father had telephoned to make sure they wouldn't be interfering with the FBI probe.

"Oh, come here, darlin'." Sally wrapped her in her arms as she hugged Faith so tight she almost lost her breath.

When they parted, Sally examined Daniel from his head to his boots.

"My, my my, Faith, Sweetheart. This sugar buns your new boyfriend?"

Faith blushed. Daniel too.

"No, he's here to perhaps work at the farm and give my folks a hand with things."

"Well, young man," Sally said as she took hold of Daniel's hand and shook it, "you mess with a hair on this young lady's head and you'll have me to deal with, and I don't play fair. No, sir. I don't play fair. This here is one angel lady who is worried sick for her granny. And you best be the perfect gentleman. I got my eyes on you, yessir, I do."

"Sally, it's okay. Honest. He is being very nice. Offered to drive me so I wouldn't have to drive in the dark."

"You going back tonight?"

"I'm going to stay as long as it takes. I need to go

through her room, please. Is everyone gone for the day?"

"Um, hum. They is." She still didn't take her eyes off Daniel, assessing whatever it was she was calibrating.

"We're going to go through her things, and we'll put everything back," said Faith.

"Well, you go right ahead. If you need anything, I'll be right over at the charge desk now. And, Son," she motioned with her two fingers from her eyes to his eyes, back and forth several times.

"Geez. Everyone here is crazy, Faith."

"A good kind of crazy," she said as she walked to her grandmother's doorway, removed the yellow crime scene tape, and opened the door.

"Oh, that's right. Of course," he mumbled and followed her inside.

The search had left much of the room in disarray. Her grandmother would never have left it like this, Faith thought. Always so neat and tidy, she made her bed every morning. She even ate the same thing for breakfast and lunch every day. She arranged her clothes on the chair the night before and always chose the nightie she was going to wear before Sally came to help her shower and get ready for bed. She never forgot where she put anything and never liked clutter. Faith remembered some arguments sometimes when she'd come to stay with them. Granny was always getting after Grandpa Frank for making a mess. She wouldn't go to bed unless the house was cleaned, fully vacuumed, and dusted.

All these little things began to add up. There actually was a lot about her grandmother she didn't really know.

"Where do you want me to start?" he asked.

"Sit right there." She pointed to the bed. "Actually, why don't you make the bed while you're at it. And then just sit and let me go through a few things first. I might have you sort stuff."

Daniel sighed loudly, which made Faith stand up straight and give him a glare.

"Sorry. I keep forgetting you're touchy."

"Touchy? You actually said touchy?"

"Faith, stop it. I didn't mean it that way." He came over to her and put his hands on her shoulders.

"You were making fun of me," she said as huge tears began to roll down her cheeks.

He tenderly wiped them away. "Hey there. No worries. You've had a lot to process. I'm being too flippant of your situation, and I apologize. Truce?"

She looked down. He used his fingers to lift her chin up.

"Come on, truce? At least for ten minutes or so?"

There it was again. He was making fun of her, but in spite of herself, she wiggled from his grip, gave him a soft slap across the arm, and said, "Okay, it's a truce then."

He went to work on the bed while Faith sorted through the things on her grandmother's desk.

She sifted through various papers, among them some requests for bloodwork, routine screenings, and copies of medical reports. Nothing there seemed out of the ordinary.

Examining each of her romance novels, Faith checked about twenty books, looking inside the cover flap, the pages, and the back cover of each. She hoped to find a piece of paper, something hidden, but found nothing.

Inside her tiny middle drawer, the rows of pens, pencils, and highlighters, along with paperclips, stickers, and tape, all were in order. She lifted each of the containers to look underneath and found nothing again. The two drawers on the right also contained files, neatly standing, an A-Z folder for paying or sorting bills, and a camera Faith didn't recognize.

She held it up. It was an old Brownie one-touch camera, very old, probably as old as her grandmother.

"What do you have there?" Daniel asked, leaning

back on the freshly made bed watching her. Faith noticed he'd removed his boots first.

"I've never seen this."

"Does it have film in it?" he asked.

"I don't know. Should I open the back?"

"You'll expose the film." He got up and examined it. He shook it, and they both heard something shaking inside. "That's not film."

Faith took it from him, slipping the black plastic lock back to open position, and removed the back of the camera. Inside was a small folded piece of paper.

She handed the camera to Daniel and then unfolded the paper.

It was a San Diego address and phone number. The name at the top was James Turner, and it wasn't her grandmother's handwriting.

Chapter 15

Annie Carr

SWEET ROMANCE AUTHOR

FAITH CALLED HER parents before they left the home.

"That's the name Tom had down at the office in Nashville. I don't know how long ago that was, but at least now we have an address. We'll get the son-of-a-bitch," her father said. "Good work."

"What if she kept it for another reason? Suppose he meant something to her?"

"And she never told you, your mother, or your siblings? Never told her sister? Nah. Who knows why she kept this. Maybe she was secretly planning revenge of some kind."

"Why do you always think the worst in people? Dad, this has got you all twisted."

"Because I know men. I know how they think sometimes. And I think your granny was a very trusting person—too trusting. You're a lot like her."

Faith didn't like hearing that.

Daniel was pacing up and down the polished floor of the central hallway in front of Sally's critical eye. Her other eye was in the middle of one of the romance novels she'd borrowed from Faith's grandmother.

"I want to come back tomorrow when we have more light. We'll head over to Morganville and then get here early. Do you know if anyone is coming? It's Saturday."

"I'm guessing not."

"I'll let you know if I hear anything."

"Fair enough. Oh, and tell Daniel his friends are good workers. I've already put them to work moving some plants. We sold a ton of trees today. It was a very good day."

"That's great, Dad. I'll tell him."

Daniel was pleased with the report. She gave him directions to her grandmother's old house, down the windy ridge of the mountain from Beersheba Springs to the flat country at the base, Morganville being the first small town that appeared. It boasted a post office, an all-purpose grocery, hardware store, and pet supply store.

He watched the little sign go by. "Population sixty-eight. Is that right?"

"In the town limits. More in the area around Morganville."

"Makes Beersheba Springs look like a big city."

"Population four hundred something. That's huge!" Faith said, chuckling.

She directed him to turn into the long driveway through dense trees. At last they came to the house, looking just as it did earlier in the week when she was here.

"Needs a little fixing up," he said as he turned off the motor. "The House of Horrors!" he imitated a creepy voice.

"Oh, stop it. It's not that creepy. Not in the day-time, anyway. This is a house with wonderful memories."

"You have to admit—"

She interrupted him. "We've had tenants off and on after they moved into the home. Raised four kids here. I used to love coming for visits. I think I came more often than any of my sisters or brother. Grandpa Frank was a country doctor, and he made house calls until he was eighty. When he started having issues with his driving, he retired, but only reluctantly."

"How long's he been gone?"

"Last year. They had a 'suite' over at the home. They liked it there because all of his old patients could visit him. He was very popular. Kind, a very special man. I loved him dearly. It was like pulling teeth to get her to move over to her own place across the hall. She had a hard time disposing of his things. It was hard on us, too."

"The house has a lot of character. Well, should we check-in then? See what's for dinner?"

They brought the gear inside, pointed to the living room where Daniel could spread out the sleeping bags. Faith sorted out the camping stove, pots, and utensils for warming the stew. Daniel had thought to ask for some large containers of water, which was a good thing, since the water had been turned off or perhaps the well had frozen again. That meant no shower, no toilet, but the home was not far away, and they could use the showers there.

Daniel spread out the sleeping bags and the foam pads, fluffing out the pillows.

"Can I ask you why we're not using the beds upstairs?" he asked.

"We have little critters who get into everything. Mice love couches. Love tearing apart mattresses, but there's another small table out on the back porch if you want to bring that in."

As he did so, he walked past her bubbling cauldron. "Smells fantastic. Didn't realize I was so hungry."

She served up two bowls of the stew, added some

squares of cornbread she'd wrapped in foil, and handed him a fork and spoon.

"Bon appetite!" she said. "Sorry about no butter for the cornbread."

"You're forgiven. Did you happen to bring some of that apple pie?"

"As a matter of fact—" She pointed to a plastic container with two slices in it. "No ice cream, and coffee in the morning will have to be black."

"Fine by me. I can see you like this."

"Summers we used to camp out all the time in the field below. Grandpa would pitch a tent. Granny would stay out with me if I was alone. We'd watch the stars all night long. Beautiful here. You can hear the trees, sometimes some coyotes, owls. More so later when it gets warmer."

"It's a shame they let this house go. It could be beautiful," he said. "Has good bones."

"Yup."

They bedded down early, but because of no light, it seemed much later than it really was. Faith knew the sleeping bags, which were rated to be used directly in the snow, would keep them warm. She was just about to slip off to sleep when Daniel asked her a question.

"What do you think happened to her, now that you have that paper?"

"I feel like I'm peering into her past, her life. I want to know the grandmother she showed me. This one, the one who runs away and has secrets, I'm not sure about. She must have had a reason."

"What's your guess?"

"I think he meant something to her. Something she couldn't tell anyone about. It's kind of sad, really, when you think about it. We didn't know that part of her. But maybe that's what she wanted. She wanted to move on."

"Yeah," he agreed. "I think the same thing. Except maybe he couldn't just move on."

"It had to have happened way before my mother's time, before she married Grandpa Frank. That's a long time to wait."

"Maybe he loved her. Really loved her. Maybe she was always a part of his life, even though they lived thousands of miles away."

"I hope you're right, Daniel. I really do."

"Pretty good for a city slicker, aren't I?"

She turned, smiling at him. "You're beginning to grow on me.

The next morning, Faith got to experience using the forest as her outhouse. She got a huge spider bite on her butt for her effort. The big red itchy bump was going to make it so she didn't forget to ask her parents to either turn the water back on or get the well checked. And she was going to suggest that perhaps Daniel and his buddies might help her clean the place up a little. If they were going to rent it out, the property had to look way more presentable.

"How'd you sleep?" he asked her on the way over to the rest home.

"Pretty good. At least I was warm enough. And it was quiet. I'd forgotten how silent the woods are in these parts. No sirens, helicopters, traffic, not even a dog bark. We didn't have any coyotes either. How about you?"

"I slept hard. I think you're right. Very quiet out here. I am looking forward to a hot shower."

"Oh man, yes." Faith decided not to tell him about her spider bite.

One of the staff members gave them each towels and soap and showed them to the staff and family shower areas. She even found some shampoo for Faith.

A young LVN motioned for Faith to come over to the desk. She was holding a book encased in a plastic gallon-sized bag, sealed. Faith recognized it as one of her grandmother's—the one that Sally had been reading.

"She said to return this to you and to be careful with it. She told me you should open it very carefully."

Daniel was right at her side when she opened the bag, pulled out the book, and studied the cover. A half-naked man was lying back, propped against a bedframe, like he was waiting for someone, a sultry, dangerous look on his face.

"Billionaires. She loved billionaires."

"Your grandma?" he asked her.

"Over half those books in there are about billionaires. It's a thing."

"Sounds crazy."

"Well, you don't read romance. They're voracious."

"I like mystery, sci-fi. Sometimes a good western." He watched her open the front cover flap. "She's written something there," he said.

In her grandmother's handwriting was a message to Sally:

'Hope you enjoy this read as much as I did. Can you imagine the adventure? Be sure to read the whole book, Sally. You don't want to miss a moment of the magic.'

And then she signed her name. Rebecca Lawler.

"Hmm. How strange. I don't—"

Out of the back of the book fell an envelope with Sally's name on it. Inside, Faith pulled out a note.

'Tell them I love them all and not to worry. I have to do something I've wanted to do for decades. I will return and will tell everyone about my adventures!'

This note was also signed by her.

"The note we were looking for, Faith. Now we can stop worrying. You were right. We both were right!" he said.

"Did she read this?" Faith looked at the young nurse.

"She was reading it when I came on this morning. She tucked it inside the book in the bag and told me to give it to you. She told me not to give it to anybody but you."

Chapter 16

Annie Carr

SWEET ROMANCE AUTHOR

I REMEMBER EVERYTHING about that day. It was warm and got warmer the more south we headed. He fiddled with the radio as we moved from town to town until, finally, he just turned it off. He gave up trying to find something consistent.

He must have known I was nervous because he didn't press me on why I hadn't said a word. I just watched the scenery, how the blue water of the lakes and canals in Florida began to peek around the green trees, how the clouds were bigger, exploding into massive displays of cotton candy. I spotted license plates from all over the US, especially from the upper east coast, places I'd never been like New York and Pennsylvania. I concentrated on all the different makes and models of cars. It all felt new, different. Like I had entered a strange new world.

At sunset, he pulled into a drive-in burger palace

where the waitresses came up to the window on roller skates, placing a tray on the ledge, and took our order, just like in the movies. I had the best chocolate shake I'd ever had. Beach Boys music blared from loud speakers hung outside under the eaves.

He watched me eat my hamburger and fries.

"What?" I asked.

"You. Just looking at you. I'm glad you came. Any regrets?"

I didn't dare tell him I was nervous as hell. "I'm fine."

"Fine. Well, you are that, Rebecca. You're very fine indeed."

I couldn't help but blush. I found it hard to look at him, as if there was some invisible ice barrier between us. We'd been so familiar before, but several weeks had gone by since those days at the coast. Now, it was like he was a stranger, and I had to start all over again.

Except he wasn't a stranger. But I still couldn't shake that apprehension of what I was doing and the excitement at being the captain of my own ship, doing something because I wanted to do it. Not what I was told.

And yes, maybe I was also excited I was doing something forbidden. Then again, I had full control over this. Or did I?

Oh, it was no use. I felt like an ice princess, sitting on a frozen throne, unable to move.

He said he'd rented a place near where we had stayed before. It was one thing to be down here with my girlfriends. But staying in a house alone with him, that did make me nervous. But I was also electrified.

I kept reminding myself I trusted him. I knew he was going to try to make me happy. I did need more than a little convincing. Without the safety net of my friends and his friends, would being alone with him change how I felt about him? I wasn't sure what I was feeling, to be honest.

Still frozen in my seat, I heard him say he thought we should find a motel for the night and finish the drive the next day.

I agreed, and so we pulled into the Flamingo Hotel, not anything like the one in Las Vegas, I'm sure, but it had a bright pink rotating neon flamingo sign in front. It looked clean, was dotted with palm trees, and had a huge turquoise swimming pool that looked inviting.

Had I brought my suit? Relieved, I realized yes, I did.

I'd even brought my flannel nightie, and I intended to keep it on. All night.

The room had an air conditioner parked in the window opening that rattled so much it made the mirror over the dresser wobble. It smelled like cigarettes, but it was clean. And there was one bed. Just one.

He probably was dying of laughter, because I went into the bathroom to change into my nightie, and I put some socks on, because that's how I liked to sleep. My feet got cold, even in the Florida heat. I had brushed my teeth and my hair, and I was ready for bed. I probably looked like a high schooler, but I was only a year out. I couldn't go to bars in Florida, whereas there were a few in Tennessee I could sneak into.

I felt like an awkward child. The fear in my belly, the realization of what I'd done, committed to even in discussing marriage, suddenly descended upon me. There was no romance in my head, not in my steps as I headed for the bed, as I climbed in and pulled the covers up to my chin.

And all the time, he watched me, smiling.

I slowly rolled over on my side, not facing him, and curled up in a ball. I really missed my home, my family, all the things I was familiar with. This wasn't me. Being scared to death wasn't an adventure. It was agony.

He turned off the lights, came back to bed, and stroked the back of my head.

"May I hold you?"

I said yes.

He slipped his body to spoon against mine, put his arm around my waist, pulled me into him, found my hands folded beneath my chin, and laced his fingers with mine.

"Goodnight, Rebecca. Sweet dreams."

I WOKE UP with a start, suddenly aware I was in a strange place. I was alone in the bed. His bag was still there on the dresser, but he was gone. I opened the door and saw the truck was also gone.

I decided to take advantage of the privacy and took a shower. I was nearly dressed when he burst through the doorway and brought me an orange juice, some coffee, and something that smelled delicious wrapped in foil.

"Morning," he said as he leaned over to me and gave me a kiss. I was, of course, still holding the towel over my exposed bra. Quickly, I slipped on my tee and joined him on the bed.

"What is this?" I asked as I pointed to the foil packet.

"It's an egg sandwich made with a fresh biscuit. This place around the corner is called Bunny's Biscuit Bar, and they make the best biscuits in Florida. Their specialty for breakfast has an egg, cheese, and a piece of bacon. You'll make me buy ten more when you taste it.

Go ahead."

He shoved one nearly in my face. He'd been completely right. The dang thing melted my insides. With my belly full of hot buttery cheese and egg goodness, my spirits improved dramatically.

"Thank you. This is out of this world!"

"See? Didn't I tell you?"

After we finished, he told me we'd be at the Gulf in about five hours.

"I've already called my boss and told him I was going to be late. He's cool with it. But, as lovely as this suite is here at the legendary Flamingo, we have to get going."

"I'm packed. I'm fed. I'm good to go," I answered him.

Nearly five hours to the minute, we pulled up to the familiar neighborhood we'd stayed at in the middle of Sunset Beach. The house was tiny, much smaller than the ones we'd stayed at before, but it was decorated with cute beachy décor. Even the light covers were shaped like angel fish. The bath curtain looked like an aquarium.

What the house might have lacked in grandeur, the view from the living room of the ocean and the white sand beach that went on forever made up for it. I'd forgotten how breathtaking it was. I felt my cares begin to melt away, replaced with pure joy.

The magic had started.

He quickly took a shower and instructed me to hang out on the beach, walk to some of the shops, or maybe get some staples for the kitchen. The kiss he gave me this time lingered long enough so that I felt the bunching in my stomach and the ache in delicious places.

It was a warning sign. And I didn't even care.

I picked up some fresh fish, some salad fixings, cream and coffee, and an assortment of fruit. I also bought bottled water but, of course, couldn't get any alcohol.

Stowing all this in the refrigerator, I then put on my suit and went out to re-acquaint myself with the beautiful ocean. I collected shells, took an old, rusty lawn chair from the side of the house, and sat with my feet into the surf, watching the water and the kids frolicking in it. I missed my big floppy hat and decided I'd get one again, but I did bring my sunglasses.

The hot part of the day was dissipating, but the sun had worn me out, so I came back inside and took a nap.

I woke up when I heard the front door slam. I rolled over just as my handsome, sweaty roommate with all the bulging muscles and tanned kissable skin leaned into my doorway, begging for my attention.

I was a little bit hungry myself.

We spent the afternoon watching the orange glow of sunset in each other's eyes, kissing slowly, and exploring with great anticipation for the progression of our relationship to come. He kissed me places I'd never been kissed. I trembled at his touch.

He wasn't yet, but I was certain he was going to be my first. And I hoped and prayed that it would last forever, that our love would be stronger than the headwinds I knew would be coming from my family by the time our week was over.

Chapter 17

Annie Carr

SWEET ROMANCE AUTHOR

IT HAD BEEN three days. When he worked, I walked the beach, looking for unusual pieces of shells and sea glass, or lay out and enjoyed the luxury of falling asleep under my new, indispensable floppy yellow hat.

My dreams were vivid. I felt his eyes on me everywhere I went, even though I knew he was working. I found myself checking the clock when it was nearing time for him to return home. The anticipation had been building, and I knew I was close to making the decision, although he had been true to his word and never pressured me.

I probably was beginning to pressure him.

Each time we got so close to falling over the edge together and didn't, I trusted him more. I probably also drove him crazy. But he didn't complain.

Tonight, when he came home, I followed him into the shower. His hands on my body and his kisses at the back of my neck sent my ears buzzing. I placed my palms against his hands as they soaped off my belly, my thighs, my chest.

"I love you, Rebecca," he whispered to the side of my face. "Marry me. I want you to be my wife. Can you see that, Sweetheart? Can you see all the days we'll have together?"

He held my head between his hands and stared into mine, pulling me to him, owning me in every way but one. I knew he knew it. I had no resistance.

"Tell me you'll marry me," he whispered again. "I need to know before I go. Please."

Of course, the only answer was, "Yes."

IT WASN'T ANYTHING like I'd imagined making love would be. My complete abandonment of myself, pouring out everything I had, matching his passion, needing more and giving more all at the same time—it truly was magic. I reveled in how it felt to bring him pleasure. I melted with the intensity of his desire to pleasure me.

We were transported to some place of our mutual choosing. We were not in Florida anymore. We weren't really there, climbing over each other on the sweaty sheets. It was someplace else without time and space, a place without boundaries, only with possibilities. I saw the days string out before me like a fine strand of pearls, the trajectory of my life sliding along that strand.

It was impossible, what was happening. It was divorced from reality, from time. It existed in this magic bubble, passion driving us forward, sustaining and keeping us warm, the ebb and flow of energy, light, and endless possibilities. There was no logic to it, no balance, no beginning or end.

It just was. No denying our connection, deeply embedded in my soul, something I would never be without ever again. I would have him in my arms for the rest of my life, no matter where he was or what danger he faced. My love would bring him home, and this would be our life together—something I never thought would happen or could happen this way.

I was certain I could withstand anything to be with him. And I'd do it lovingly, because I was loved so deeply, so completely.

The last day of our paradise was not a work day for him. We readied the house for tomorrow's turnover, had an early dinner, and walked out onto the beach to watch the last sunset. Tomorrow was the road trip, the meeting with my family, the parting for now.

But not before the beautiful union of our bodies in the bright shadow of the dying sun. I poured out all the rest of what remained of the old me, and he filled me with joy and pure Heaven.

When we drove up the driveway to my parents' home, my father was on the porch. He wasn't a violent man, but I could see he was seething with anger, his fists made into hard twisted weapons if he chose to use them. A man of the cloth, I knew what he felt, how it would be an indictment of everything he'd been teaching me and his whole flock for these past twenty years or more. His daughter violated his trust as she found trust in another.

James tried to speak, but my dad cut him off.

"I am going to have you arrested. She's a minor."

"Sir, I mean her no harm. We are in love."

"No, she isn't old enough to love you. You can't love a child."

"Dad! I'm not a child."

He stared at me as if I'd hit him across the face. "Go inside. We'll talk about this, but after this person is gone from my property."

"James, his name is James. And I love him. I'm going to marry him, Dad. We love each other. We're committed—"

He nearly hit me. It was the first time in my whole life I ever feared he'd hurt me. But he held back, maybe sensing James wouldn't stand for it.

He turned and faced my beloved. "You did this."

"I did," he admitted. "Yes, it is my responsibility. I I-love her."

"I have filed the paperwork. I'm going to arrest you. My wife has learned you are going into the Navy from one of her friends. Is this true?"

"Yes. I report in two days."

"Then I won't interfere with your naval career, but you will not interfere with her future. With ours, as a family. You are not to see her or talk to her until you are out. If she still wants to see you after, then and only then will I tear up the paperwork. But if you think it's worth ruining your life over this, ruining her life over this, this stunt you've pulled—I don't care whether you call it love or not. You've probably violated my daughter, made her unclean!"

"That's not—"

"Are you married to her or not?"

"No, I'm not. But—"

"Are you more than five years older than she is?"

"Yes."

"Is she a minor?"

"She is."

"Then, young man, you've raped her. I can and will have you arrested. I will see to it that your commanding officer knows about this. You'll be booted from the

Navy and will spend some time in prison. I have powerful friends here. Now, go and don't come back until you've finished your obligation. If you can finish that, then and only then can you consider having my daughter."

I sank to my knees. I heard my mother approach from behind.

"Oh, Child, I'm so sorry," she whispered.

I stiffened. Looking up to my father, I screamed, "I hate you!"

Dad turned to James. "See? You see what you've done? I'm left with the pieces after you've had your fun."

"I'm telling you it wasn't like that."

"I don't care what you're telling me. What I'm telling you is that you have a choice. What you've done is irreparable. Look at what you've turned my daughter into. She now says she hates me, but of course, she loves you. You had no right to turn her head like this."

"I will honor and protect her. I am committing to her and her alone. I'm an honorable man, sir."

"Your choice is simple. If you're an honorable man, you decide then. Which is it to be? Will you be an honorable man in the Navy or will you be an honorable man in prison? You choose. Go ahead, think about what that will do to her, visiting you behind bars. Knowing you've ruined both your lives. You have a choice. Choose wisely!"

James looked at me in shock. I had no answer for him, except the regret I felt that I hadn't warned him about my dad. Yet I'd never seen this before. The thought of him in prison, arrested for rape of all things, destroyed me. It would be known by the whole town. It would be in the papers, my sisters and brother forever shamed. I would stand by him, no matter what. But if we had a chance, it was only to bear a separation until he was done with his service.

I could wait. Could he?

"I will wait for you, James. If it takes two years or six, I will wait for you. My life is yours, my heart is yours. I do not want you to sacrifice your career over this. We should have thought this through, and I didn't know the law, the rules, or what a monst—"

"There's your answer, Son. If your love is strong enough, it will survive. But I warn you, there is to be no communication between you whatsoever. None. Or I'll file that paperwork. It's all ready to go, waiting on your decision."

"Mine too," I said. "James, please, he means it. I don't know how we can fight this. I'm so sorry. I didn't know. I couldn't live with myself if I cause you to be charged, to lose your future over me, when I can wait. We can wait. I believe in us. I don't want to see you go to jail, not if I can help it. Please, understand me."

James' shoulders drooped. He touched the porch with his shoe, making a circle like he'd done in the sand. He looked up to me and smiled.

"Rebecca, I'll love you forever. Know that. I'll never stop loving you. If you change your mind and need to move on, I forgive you for that in advance."

He stood tall, looking down on my father. "To you, I say this. If I ever have a son or a daughter someday, I hope to God I don't dash their dreams like you've done. And for what?"

"It's the law. We're a nation of laws."

"It is. You're right. I don't have the ability to fight with you over this. She wants me to go, so I will. But know this, I hope I show more compassion and love for my son or daughter than you have here. And if you can live with yourself, so be it. I'll abide by your wishes. And we'll see what the future holds for all of us."

"James," I said, running to him. Nothing was going to stop me from hugging him. I cried into his chest. He held me, and I could feel him shaking too.

"I mean what I say, Rebecca. It's all good. I'll love you forever, always. What we found can never be lost."

My whole world was torn upside down. I flew into the house, nearly tripping over my bag with the floppy yellow hat on top.

Chapter 18

SWEET ROMANCE AUTHOR

"I'M PREGNANT."

My mother put the stack of Vacation Bible School booklets down on the table.

"Are you sure?"

"Of course I'm sure. There's no mistaking when I *got* pregnant. I haven't had a period for two months now. My clothes are fitting more tight."

She sat down. Hard. Placing her forehead into her hand, she began to cry. I was the one who should be crying. I honestly didn't want to gear up for another fight with my father, and lately, these had been happening almost daily.

"We should get a blood test, Rebecca. Let's make sure first, and then we'll tell your dad."

"What does this mean?"

"I don't think you'll be going away to college this fall."

"Will he reconsider what he threatened? I need to tell James. Maybe Dad will let me marry him without filing that paperwork. We can do it if you give permission. Or I could apply as an emancipated minor, but—"

"We'll find out first, and then we'll discuss it."

The results were positive. So we set up the discussion on an evening when my younger sisters and brother were gone.

"It's simple. You'll get married."

"To James?" I had a semblance of hope still.

"No. That's still ongoing. He's got another obligation to fulfill first. It doesn't work like that. He has to stay in, but you, on the other hand, your life—all our lives will be forever altered by this child. So you should get married."

"But I don't want to get married. I'm waiting for my—"

"You won't have this baby out of wedlock. The baby needs a father."

"But James, James is the father."

"But James isn't here. Don't you see, Rebecca? He even said it himself. If you have to move on, then do it."

"But I don't want to move on."

"Becca, he's not tried to contact you, right?"

"No, because you said—"

"He still violated the law."

"Lots of people get married younger than twenty. That's not very young anymore. Parents give permission all the time for this."

My mother stuck up for me. "Let her try to reach him. Think of how you'd feel if someone kept your baby from you."

To my surprise, my dad relented. I spent the next several days trying to find James. I was given a number to call so I could leave a message for him, but he didn't call back. I inquired again and was told that he wasn't in that particular unit. Then I was told he'd been shipped out on a destroyer on rotation, which didn't make sense. He hadn't finished Basic.

Then I was told he'd been involved in a training accident. I was told he wasn't on the roster and then was told he was listed as deceased. At every step, I was warned that due to security concerns, they would neither confirm or deny his enlistment in the Navy. They suggested I call other branches of service.

My father had a friend who worked in the recruiter's office, and once again, word came back that he was deceased. I spent a whole week in bed after I got that news. My father finally apologized to me, said he regretted standing in the way. Of course, by then, it was way too late. I never forgave him for that.

But I was determined to move on. Not having the baby was out of the question for us. No matter what had happened to James, I wanted this baby, and I wasn't going to put it up for adoption.

I knew that tongues would wag if the community saw the pastor's daughter pregnant with no husband in sight. But I wasn't even dating anyone. My situation was hopeless. I decided, and began planning to move away, have the baby, and start a new life somewhere near Nashville.

But it was hard. I was looking for work, as well as dealing with the reality of James' death. I felt myself sink into a deep depression. I was alienated from my family and had no one to turn to.

My father's friend Dr. Frank Lawler was a traveling country doctor who made house calls. And when told of my condition, he agreed to see me. He also agreed to be my physician for the pregnancy until I relocated and had moved out of the house.

I remember the day he stopped by. He'd been a member of Dad's church, but in recent years, his practice had built up and he wasn't attending regularly. My father, of course, made a comment about it.

Dr. Frank was gentle as he examined me. We talked about what I was eating, my lack of sleep, and how he didn't want to prescribe anything because of the pregnancy.

"I'm so sorry about your loss, Rebecca. No wonder you feel depressed. Facing raising this child all alone is a big responsibility. Losing the man you love—well, there isn't any way to fix that. But you're smart, gifted, so your mother says. I'm sure you'll be able to manage, but it will take time."

I was grateful he didn't judge me. We agreed to meet weekly, discuss what was going on, while he gave me suggestions of things I could do to keep busy. He offered to give me a part-time job in his office to help pay the expenses I was saving for the relocation.

As the weeks went by, we became friends. He was twenty years my senior and had been engaged once. Tragically, his fiancé had passed away many years ago from an aggressive cancer. We had that in common. Our friendship grew stronger.

One day, he surprised me.

"I've been thinking about your situation. I hope you don't think I'm being presumptuous, but I've grown very fond of you, Rebecca, and I think we make a good team. Would you consider marrying this old country doctor? I promise to love and care for your little one just as if he was mine. And if you're willing, I'd like to have more children, the two of us together.

Our children."

I was amused because his proposal absolutely petrified him. I knew he'd been rehearsing it over and over again, and in the heat of the moment, he'd forgotten some of his lines.

He was well-respected by everyone and had done relatively well for himself. I could complete one piece of his life where there had been an ugly pain, black hole. There was a void in my life too. I'd thrown caution to the winds, and the consequences were weighing on me. Maybe we needed each other in some special way that would solve all our problems.

I knew I could grow to love him in time. I was honest with him for what I felt and didn't feel. But I promised to honor and obey him, to give him the best of what I had in exchange for his love and devotion to my unborn child. I even had the feeling that James, if he were still alive, would approve.

We had a very simple ceremony in my parents' church attended by only a handful of people. Our wedding night was tender and beautiful, and I had no regrets. I hoped he didn't either.

When our daughter was born, he moved us into the house he'd received in a settlement. Together, we fixed it up and made it a lovely, cozy home. We raised three other children.

My brother, Lou, who was going to inherit the ranch from my grandparents, was killed in Vietnam as a Navy pilot. Once, during Spring Break, we took the kids to the beach for a week, driving along the east and west coasts of Florida. I never told them I'd been here before. How my perception had changed in my years raising the children with Frank. My turn to watch out for the girls, remembering how my father felt. In a way, I relived it through their eyes now.

We drove to the east coast and stopped at a Navy memorial museum, honoring those who had fallen during Vietnam. Lou's picture was there with a group of young, handsome "hot shots," as they were called. I discretely inquired about James, even though I'd been told he'd passed early in his training, stateside.

The guide looked up what could have been his years of service and discovered he did serve for six years. He was discharged from the elite unit he'd joined in 1971. When I told him the erroneous news I'd received years ago, the guide shrugged, promised me he'd look into it.

True to his word, he telephoned me a week later.

"There was a James Turner who died in a skydiving accident in 1964. It wasn't combat related. He was taking his first solo jump on a weekend off."

James had always talked about fate. Maybe it was

for the best. I was glad he'd lived more years than I'd been told. I hoped he'd been happy.

As I thought on it, life had presented me with a series of riddles and inexplicable dark times and wonderful golden possibilities. In the end, I got what I always wanted: true love, a man who loved me with all his heart, a family of my own with someone there to raise and love them as much as I did, parents who became proud of me and were a part of my life and the lives of our children. I had it all, just not in one package.

And maybe James' story wasn't over yet.

I hoped one day I'd find out.

Chapter 19

SWEET ROMANCE AUTHOR

"Sʜᴇ's ᴄᴏᴍɪɴɢ ʙᴀᴄᴋ?"

Faith handed her mother the note she'd pulled from the back of the romance novel. "Look at this, Mom."

"Oh my God. Have you any idea what this is?" she said as she looked at the two of them.

"You should ask her, because well, we've been talking, and—" Daniel had been interrupted by Faith's mother's horrified look.

She didn't react very wisely. "And since when are you the judge and jury on this family? How dare you assume you know anything about our family. And this, I mean, you're here to look at the nursery, not to get involved in our family life."

"Oops," Daniel said as he looked down at his feet, rounding his shoulders like replicating a turtle going back into his shell.

Faith didn't appreciate that at all. "Mother, he drove me down there. You gave permission for that. You knew we were looking for clues, and we found this note this morning. We drove straight back up here to give it to you—so you wouldn't worry. And this is how you treat our guest? He's been a wonderful help and a companion. We've been like, what?" Faith looked over at him, and Daniel shrugged.

"Super sleuths. It's been a regular Nancy Drew type of experience for me," Daniel said.

"Lord. O Lord, I don't know what this world is coming to. I can't believe this is happening. So tell me, where did you get this?" she asked me.

"Sally had it. She was reading it when we were there searching through the room before. She's had it ever since Granny went missing. I think Granny left it in her box the night she left. That's what Sally thinks anyway."

"Look at the inscription she left her," said Daniel.

Faith's mother read the dedication. "Whatever does she mean by that?"

Faith's father had an opinion. "Well, it looks like all those theories about her going voluntarily are true. What this doesn't explain, if it is this James person that she's gone off with, is the police report or the filing that your grandfather did, Margaret. Does it?"

"No, it doesn't. Why would Grandpa try to have someone that my mother loved arrested?"

"I think we're going to have to wait until she comes back, and maybe she'll tell us. Maybe she just had to go consult with someone, see a counselor, or something. I don't know. But if she went off with him, then I think they might have been in love. Maybe they're still in love," Faith said.

Her dad put his hands on his hips. "But she's eighty years old! You're telling me that she runs off with some strange man and she's eighty years old? Surely this isn't about sex." His nose was wrinkled, and he was bothered by the lack of logical answers.

Daniel had an answer for that, and Faith regretted what she was going to hear.

"Eighty years old? That's not old. I mean, my grandparents—"

All three held their hands out and stopped Daniel's further explanation.

"Okay, okay, I get it. But just don't think you guys are the experts on aging. What's the matter with people having sex when they're eighty and ninety years old? It happens you know."

Faith knew what the problem was. The problem was nobody saw Granny as a sexual object. And perhaps that was a big mistake. But nobody wanted to hear it.

"Daniel, please. No more about your grandparents."

Faith could hear the phone ringing in the house. Her dad left to go answer it.

"Oh, I forgot to tell you, Faith. There's a woman who called earlier and said she would call back. She's an older lady, a former friend of your granny's. She wanted to know about the party. I told her she'd have to talk to you."

"Okay." Then, at a distance, Faith heard her father calling her.

"Faith, you have a phone call. It's one of your grandmother's friends. About the party?"

She ran to the kitchen and grabbed the phone.

"Hello?"

"Oh, sweetheart, this is Savannah Cutler, and I'm an old friend of your grandmother's."

"Nice to meet you. What can I do for you? You are interested in the party?"

"Well, yes. She and I were schoolmates, and her mother and my mother were the biggest gossips in Lynchburg that ever were. I mean, they stayed in touch, bless their hearts, until the day they died. Your grandmother and I used to commiserate a lot about our mothers. And I saw the article written about

Rebecca's 80th birthday party. I'm married and moved to Georgia, and I haven't seen your grandmother in, oh, years and years and years. I know that she got married to a country doctor, Doc Lawler. But I haven't seen her in all that time, and I just wanted to ask your permission if I could attend her birthday party. It would mean a lot to me, Dear."

"Oh, I think she probably would love that." But the shadow had come over Faith as she wondered about telling her grandmother's friend about what was happening with her right now.

"I need to ask you a question, if I may?"

"Sure. Anything."

"We hope we're still having the party," Faith started.

"Oh dear? Is she all right? Is she sick or ill?"

"As far as we know, she's fine. But she's gone missing, and we're trying to locate her."

"Oh my God. I can't believe it. Did she wander away from the rest home? I understand that's where she's living now."

"No, we think she left voluntarily."

"Oh dear. That's bad news. I'm so sorry."

"Well, that leads to another question." Faith bit her lip and continued. "Do you know anything about someone named James? James Turner?"

"Oh, James! What a handsome young man he was, Faith. Your grandmother was smitten with him. And I have to say, he could hardly take his eyes from her either. We were just sure that someday they'd be together, and frankly, I was very surprised when she married Doc Lawler, although he'd been a great catch and out there for many years. Many, many women had chased him over the years or at least so it was that my mother told me. But James, he was head over heels for your grandmother. And his eyes. I still remember those gorgeous blue eyes."

"You see, Savannah, none of us have ever heard anything about him."

"I see where you're going with this. Well, you know a woman's heart is kind of a private thing."

"So you're saying she has secrets. Secrets you know about, but we don't."

"I don't know what happened between them. We always wondered because they were so happy together. Maybe he called it off when he went into the Navy. Men did that back then, you know. Or it might be that she decided marrying the doctor was more stable. He was also very handsome. Very popular, a very good doctor. She made a good choice, Faith. You can be assured of that."

"Yes, she loved my grandpa, still does."

"A woman has to choose what is going to be her life's path. We don't always know what's in a woman's heart, do we? Poets and philosophers have wondered about that and about the stars in equal measure, Faith. I think perhaps James just moved on. That's what I think."

"We thought it odd she never mentioned him, even after Grandpa died."

"But *we* always wondered, and it was funny because two of my friends, Ashley and Penny, they also married doctors. None of us live in Lynchburg anymore. They would love to see her too. Although I suppose you have a limit of how many people can come."

"No, I think we're good. I don't have time to send them an invite, if we do have the party, that is. So give them the information. My biggest problem now is whether I'm going to have a guest of honor."

"Say, why are you asking me about James, exactly?"

"Well, we think they might be together somewhere. And I was just wondering, do you have any idea where they could be?"

"You mean together, as in today?"

"Yes, that's what I mean."

There was a long pause on the other end of the phone. After several seconds, she sighed. "Have you tried the Gulf Coast of Florida?"

"Florida?"

"Yes, the Sunset Beach area. On the Gulf of Mexico. If I had a million dollars to bet, I'd look for her there. But that's just a guess from an eighty-one-year-old woman who has far more crazy ideas than good ones. But I think that could be where she's gone, uh, where they've gone if he's with her. And I don't think she's the kind of person, unless she's changed, to not let you know. That surprises me."

"She did leave a note with her caregiver, left strategically after she had already gone, and she said she'd be back in a week. Do you believe that?"

"Oh, Faith, you sound like you're very young. Wait till you get to be my age, Sweetheart. I don't want to step on any parenting toes, but I've told my girls many, many times over the years that affairs of the heart just have their own path, don't they? You just never know when you'll fall in love. And it's something that we ladies hold secret and dear to us. My husband, God rest his soul, never knew about some of the boyfriends I had. And I think it was better that way."

Chapter 20

Annie Carr

"YOU CAN'T GO to another state and arrest this fellow for a sixty-year-old inquiry or filing that was never completed or withdrawn complaint. It's interesting, but it isn't actionable," the FBI agent said.

Faith's dad was adamant that, with the record of possible rape, they could pick up this James fellow and bring him back to Nashville or Lynchburg. He was worried, he said, about his mother-in-law's safety.

"Well, one of the things that's a problem, sir," said the other agent, "is that the victim in this case is possibly willingly with him. This is not a kidnapping. He was an old boyfriend. Doesn't sound like there is any violence or coercion. The statutes expired long ago. There's no crime. She's an adult, and she went of her own free will."

"But she's eighty," said her dad.

"Well, I don't know," the agent retorted. "My

grandmother can beat me in Scrabble, Monopoly, and most card games. About the only thing she can't beat me in game-wise is chess. It just doesn't make any sense to go after him, and it ties up the FBI's resources. If you wanted to, you could call the local sheriff down there and have them detain him, but what would that do really? And what if you were wrong? What if she claims she was his willing companion? You'd just be wasting their time."

The other agent began again. "You can't all of a sudden take away her rights just because she's eighty. She has a right to go and do what she wants. She's not ruled incompetent. She certainly isn't underage, either. It's voluntary. and until she's deemed a danger to herself mentally or physically, there's really nothing we can do."

Faith was relieved to hear it.

"Mom," she started. "Let us go down. Daniel and I can go. Let's go down and see if we can find her. Maybe Savannah can give us some ideas where to look. I think if we went to the Gulf, we'd find her, and I would much rather we talk to her and see what's going on firsthand rather than sending the authorities in. It kind of seems stupid to me… Here we're planning this big 80th birthday party, but we have to bring her back in handcuffs? Put her old flame in jail? *'Happy Birthday,*

Granny, while we ruin the rest of your life?' Does that really make sense to you?"

Daniel shook his head and then chuckled. "I thought my family was full of drama queens and kings. Boy, they can't hold a hand candle to you guys."

Faith's mom looked at her husband. "Maybe all the boys could go down with Faith. You could go too, if you wanted, take a road trip down there. If all of you go have a look, I'm sure you'd find her if she's there."

"Sir, Mr. Goddard, if I could make a suggestion?" the first agent said. "I think letting the young people go down is the best bet. I think it can be handled in a way that she could possibly be convinced to return home. You want to de-escalate it. You don't want to make it too confrontational. That's why I really don't think it's a good idea to get the local sheriff involved. That would be the Pinellas County Sheriff. I know him. He's a real nice guy and an honest family man. You really don't want to get them involved. And they have a lot of other more important things to do."

Faith could see her father was beginning to cave.

The agent continued, "At this point, with this letter and her admission that she's gone somewhere to do something she's wanted for years, we have to believe this is voluntary. She told her family not to worry even. This note doesn't sound like a crazy woman or someone who is depressed or in distress. This sounds like a very determined woman who's sure about what she's doing, and to be honest with you, she sounds like she's pretty fearless, very sane, and she'd probably fight you back. You really don't want to do that. It's not the way we should treat our elders."

Faith's mother had a reaction to that. "Our elders shouldn't go running off without leaving a note either. We've been worried sick about her."

"Ma'am, see there I have to differ with you again. She left the note. She left it with Sally. And why did she leave it with Sally? Because she probably knew you guys would blow a cork. And look at you, you have."

"He's right, Mom," said Faith.

Daniel added, brightly. "Why don't I take Rodrigo and Jason and the four of us get to the Gulf? We'll watch over your daughter, sir, and I think since your mother-in-law doesn't know what we look like we might be able to fade into the woodwork somewhere and just kind of do some clandestine surveillance. She said she'd be back in a week, and that's in, what, two days?" Daniel looked at Faith. "Yeah, two days. If we leave today, we can be there by tonight, and we'll just hang out. Shoot, I've never seen the Gulf Coast, and I hear it's real pretty. We're a little short of funds, though. So if you don't mind—"

Her mother inserted herself. "Oh, heck, we can spring for a couple of motel rooms." Then she turned to the FBI agent. "Am I missing something here or do you think this is how we should handle it?"

He chuckled, and finally, the tension appeared to be broken. He stared back at her. "This isn't an official response, of course, but I think it sounds like a very sensible solution. You're just going to check out what's going on. It's like a welfare check, except it's three states away. But your grandmother is worth it, and she is not young, and you just want to make sure that she's okay. Make sure there isn't some mental aspect to this, that her state of mind hasn't gone sideways. It's always something we have to think about. But I think it's a good way to do it in a non-threatening way, and I think it sounds like she'd be happy to see Faith, at least. I don't know about the rest of you guys."

Daniel laughed, so did Rodrigo and Jason.

"Well, you never know about these California kids, do you?" said Faith.

FAITH HAULED IN her pack, returning the sleeping bags to her dad. She thanked him for all the goodies he stuck in the box and for letting them stay warm with the sleeping bag.

"About the house, Dad, I think you guys could

make some money. It would help with your finances here if you get somebody in there to rent it. It's a sweet little house. With a little bit of work, you could get a lot of money. I think Grandma would love seeing it fixed up, and who knows, maybe these guys could rent it from you in exchange for wages while they're deciding what they want to do. That way you get some handy guys working on the house, and you'd also get your workers for the farm. It sounds crazy, but I think it's a win-win. What do you say, Dad?"

Faith waited for him to give a response. "How'd you get so smart all of a sudden?" he said to her.

"I've been hanging around you and Mom a long time. And don't worry about Granny. I think she's lucky she's got a family that loves her and wants to take care of her. I think this is the best way we can show her that. But arresting the man she used to be in love with, might still be in love with?" She shook her head.

"You're right, Kid. Sounds like you're beginning to use some of those attorney skills already."

"Yeah, this type of thing, finding missing relatives elderly and young people, it's not anything I ever thought I'd be interested in. But the way all of this has unfolded, I can see how people just fall through the cracks. We're all so busy, and then life does what life does."

"Well, you better get your clothes together upstairs. I think your friend Daniel is anxious to get down to the coast. I can't say as I blame him. Your mom and I had a good time down there when we had our honeymoon. And we used to go there quite a bit before you were born. Now, of course, we're busy."

"If you had enough people helping you out, Dad, then you can go there and dream. You don't have to be a working fool all the time. You can make money, make a profit, and have your dreams. I'm for having it all, not just some of it."

Chapter 21

Annie Carr

SWEET ROMANCE AUTHOR

FAITH AND THE three guys jumped in Daniel's truck and headed off, Daniel being very slow and careful not to raise dust on the driveway, as he'd been told. Between the guys in the back seat was an ice chest filled with sandwiches, fruits, and some waters that Faith's mother had prepared for them. She hugged her parents and promised that as soon as they had a sighting of her grandmother, they would take a picture and send it to them.

Their GPS on their phones said it would take over eleven hours, but as they crossed the Florida-Georgia Line much sooner than they thought, they realized they were going to get down there in time to see the sunset. That's what everyone had told Faith about. Not to miss the sunset on the beach.

She and Daniel talked about all sorts of things. He explained what was happening with California and the farm industry, the way the family farms were being controlled. Sacramento area had been a large rice growing region, but water was scarce in the Golden State, and anything that needed lots of water, whether it was retreated or reclaimed water didn't matter, those types of industries were going to be in tough shape.

Of course, the Central Valley was drying up. All the water up north was coming down south where the largest population was. It had been that way for years, he said. He told Faith that his grandparents were surprised they'd been able to take care of the farm for as long as they did. In the end, they sold to a subdivider, who built houses on it outside of the Fresno area.

Faith told him about her experience growing up in Tennessee. She also had visited the beaches in Florida, South Carolina, and Virginia; she told him she would like someday to be close by the water, hearing that it was healthy.

"Why don't you try to take over your granny's little house?" he asked her.

"I could. I just feel somehow my destiny is elsewhere. I don't know why, but I want to be close to the ocean. I guess it just has some kind of an appeal to me. It's so different from what I have."

"Well, you can always work the farm and then take lots of vacations. I thought you gave your dad a lecture about that before we left."

"You're right. I did. And I do love the ranch. I like growing things. I love the greenhouses. I really don't mind all of the work that's involved, but I don't like the stress of having to depend on Mother Nature, and it's hard when you have a bad winter or an extra warm spring or summer. Sometimes you can't adjust fast enough, and then there's always the economy."

"Yeah, farmers have that problem, don't they? But think of it this way too, if we were selling widgets somewhere and some other country was able to sell widgets cheaper than we could make them, then we'd be in the same boat. I think what you have to do is to do what you can to make it profitable, enhance it, and make it so that it's hard work, yes, but only if you enjoy it. People shouldn't ranch if they don't enjoy ranching, and they shouldn't ranch if they're in it just for the money. You do it for your legacy; you do it for your kids. It's the way of life that we like. I thought you knew that."

Faith thought about it for several minutes, not saying a word.

"So do you like Tennessee?" she finally asked.

"From what I can see, it's pretty nice. I love the people. The countryside is beautiful. Lots to do with the hiking, fishing, music businesses, and distilleries.

It's got a rich culture we never learned about in California, so I studied up on it before we decided to come out here. So far, everything we've been told is spot on. I could be happy there. Your parents are doing a good job, though. I don't think they're ready to really retire, do you?"

"No. Now if this ranch were in Florida, well, I think I'd do just about anything to go there."

"Well, let's see, Faith. Let's see how Florida grows on you. I'm going to see it for the first time today. And I'll tell you later on."

"It's a deal." She smiled.

She had fallen asleep when they stopped to get gas. The sky was bright orange, looking like it was on fire. From inside the open driver door, Daniel yelled at her, "Won't be long now. Time to go use the restroom. We got about a half an hour to go."

Faith could hardly wait.

They came over the causeway from Tampa, headed out toward the islands where the little coastal communities and beaches were, on their way to Sunset Beach. Her mother had made a reservation at a hotel not far from the commercial district, filled with restaurants and shops and ice cream stores. The causeway gave them a beautiful view of the glassy blue ocean beyond and the laciness of the sugar sand beaches extending in a long crescent arc as far as Faith could see.

All three of the boys were mesmerized. All Daniel could say was, "Would you look at that? Isn't that just about the most beautiful thing you've ever seen in your life?"

They traveled down Gulf Boulevard until their GPS system told them to turn back north, and that's where they found the hotel. Her mother had booked two rooms side by side, the boys' room having two queen beds so they could share.

Chapter 22

Annie Carr

SWEET ROMANCE AUTHOR

I ALWAYS KNEW I would see James again—I thought either in this world or the next. And if it was the next, I had an idea that Frank would know what was in my heart, and he would understand that my love for James had never faltered, had never diminished, even while I was loving my sweet country doctor.

I knew I wasn't fooling myself. A mother can love all of her children each in their own special way, but love them the same. We love our fathers and mothers in different ways, but we love them nonetheless. I wasn't raised to have two husbands. I wasn't raised to fall in love with two men. Thank goodness I didn't have to choose one over the other, because that would've ruined my soul.

Frank was the perfect husband for me, and I explained it to James. Tears rolled down his face when I told him how much I love Frank and how grateful I was. I told him that not a day went by when I looked at Margaret, our daughter, and didn't think of him. But she was also Frank's daughter, and Frank loved her regardless of the fact that she was not his blood. And he loved our other three children just the same. It was just perfect like that.

James explained why he'd never tried to contact me. He discovered I'd married and even had another child, and didn't want to upset the life I was living. He especially didn't think my husband deserved it, nor my children either. But years later, after his own wife died, he'd tried to find me and was unsuccessful.

When my family asked me why I didn't tell them about James, I said it was because it was personal to me, the me that existed outside of the family. The me who made mistakes, was impulsive, who walked where she should not have walked, but who loved and paid the price for it. It wasn't anything that would make anyone understand or love me more, so it was something I kept to myself. I told no one except Frank. Frank knew. He had to know.

He loved me anyway.

I had an extraordinary life filled with memories, children, heartaches, and losses. I never spent any time thinking about the days we could have had together, because we had those days, as many as we deserved.

James had married and then been widowed in his sixties, never raising a family. He spent many years thinking about what could have been and, instead, threw himself into his work and became a successful contractor in California. As if he was fulfilling the promise he made to me even though I was no longer at his side, he bought the bungalow he'd been building when he met me. And he had retired to this place several years ago, when I was still raising children, raising grandchildren, and helping my parents with the church and Frank with his practice.

Later, he didn't know we'd moved into the rest home together. He'd lost track of where I was after he found out that I had married and had a brood of children. A perfect pod of four. And that was enough for him. I had a life, I was happy, and that was all there was to it.

When he told me the story of why he decided to come see me, it was my turn to cry.

"I saw this announcement in the paper in Nashville. It had been picked up, I guess, from one of the local papers where the home was. I knew you were from that general area, but I had no intention of trying to visit. I was with several friends, on a business trip, wandering around trade shows, when I saw the article. And then Faith was on TV talking about the party they were having for you for your 80th, and then I knew where you lived. I'd found you. There were no pictures of you, but I combed the articles and did a little bit of research before I went back to California and discovered that Frank had passed. My little house here at Sunset Beach I'd put into a rental pool, and I protected the month of May, your birthday month, wondering, if I showed up at your door, would you spend your birthday, your most important 80th birthday, with me?"

He was the same as he'd always been. Thoughtful, handsome, his body in remarkable shape, his silvery hair thick and shiny. And those eyes looked at me, and when he did so, I was twenty years old again on the beach in a yellow floppy hat with big sunglasses, waiting for him to come home. It all came back to me just the way he looked at me.

Faith and her friends were at the house for dinner. She managed to do a FaceTime with me and show her mother that I was well, that I was well cared for too and happy. In the background, Noel didn't look so pleased, but that was Noel. I could do lots of things, but I could not do miracles.

"Maggie, I have someone special I would like you to meet."

I saw her face, her mouth going flat in a straight

line, her eyes widen as she took in a deep breath. She swallowed.

"Okay. I'm ready."

"I'd like you to meet James." I pulled the camera to the side so she could see the both of us in the screen.

"Hi, Margaret. I'm James."

My daughter was waiting for me to give her an explanation, so I didn't delay.

"Maggie, James is your father. I was pregnant with you when I married your father, Frank. He was your real father, the man who raised you as his daughter, the man who loved you all those years. I want you to meet the man who never knew about you, who didn't interfere with our family, but who loved you all same, your biological father."

James was sweating, and I could see he was nervous. Maggie was at a total loss for words. I saw Noel hold her hand and put his arm around her shoulder.

"You can't expect that we're just going to accept this, Rebecca," he said.

"Of course not. I understand."

"So don't you think it would've been a good idea to tell people about this, this little indiscretion?"

"I'm afraid you can't ask that question anymore, the only person who deserves to give you an answer is Frank, and he's gone now. It was Frank's idea not to tell anyone, And I supported it completely. What would be the use of doing anything that would diminish the bond that was created the day you were born, Maggie? Frank was there, and he loved you every single day of his life."

I saw her cheeks glisten with streaks of tears. She had a hard time looking back into the camera. "I'm sorry, Mom, and I apologize. It's just too hard for me to accept everything right now. I'm glad you're well. So does this mean you're leaving us?"

Her eyes welled over with tears, and her lips quivered. I could see the pain in her eyes at the thought that I would forsake her for my old flame, even if he was her father.

"Absolutely not, Sweetheart. He will be as much a part of the family as you want him to be. But know this, I intend to live with him. I intend to live with him here on the Gulf Coast of Florida. This is where our love began, and this is where it will end. It's not negotiable. But I love you no less than I did before all this happened. Please understand my need to close this circle. He is part of our family, whether you accept him or not. I sincerely hope that you will."

When the call ended, I was going to fall into James' arms, but Faith grabbed me and, on her knees, buried her head in my chest.

"Oh my God, Granny, I had no idea. Please forgive me. I will do anything, anything to help bring us all together."

Her sweet face looked up at me, and I saw so much of myself in her. She even cried the same kinds of tears, and when I looked at the young man she was with whose hand she clutched tight to her side as she was kneeling in front of me, I noticed something very important.

He also had very beautiful blue eyes.

Chapter 23

Annie Carr

FAITH FINISHED ALL the decorations for the party. The multipurpose room at the home had never looked so festive. She had the boys bring in several flowering orange trees, which scented the whole area, almost making it feel like some kind of an exotic love temple. She had pulled in some draperie, and an old circus tent, which she found in a Goodwill store. It was infused with slivers of silver and golden rags, as well as colorful seams of ruffled material that looked like feathers. When she saw what they'd done, anchoring all the edges up to the corners of the room with the tall pole in the center, it looked more like a harem's palace than a multipurpose room at a rest home in a small town in Beersheba Springs, Tennessee.

Daniel had spent evenings reading about the area, reading about a woman novelist who recorded her travels throughout the area—part missionary, part seeker of adventure and fortune. She'd written several books in the latter part of the 19th century, all printed under a pseudonym with a man's name, because women couldn't be published then. He read to Faith while she made her list and checked it twice. She responded with little notes to people sending their regrets or answering emails about people traveling and where they should stay and helping them with their arrangements.

The group had started out being barely fifty, and now was well over a hundred. And Faith asked for and received lots of donations so they could throw the kind of party for Granny that she deserved. Daniel read to her something that touched her greatly.

"Listen to this, Faith. *'I have traveled in most of the South, and I have traveled some in Europe and a few countries in South America. I have walked under the buildings in San Francisco and ridden the cable cars when they were brand new. I have visited rodeos and camped with Indians in their teepees and even partook of some rituals I probably can't talk about.'"*

Faith laughed at that. "Okay, you didn't tell me this was an erotic journey. I thought you were reading something about the historical nature of this area. I'm glad my granny didn't meet her or she would have flown further off course."

"No, listen. Seriously, Faith, listen," he insisted. "There's more to it.

"*'I think you can tell when God has touched a country and a people. I feel God's hand everywhere I walk in the beautiful state of Tennessee. I have enjoyed traveling through Georgia and through North and South Carolina as well and felt similar stirrings. But I have never felt the kind of passion and romance as I felt when I walked the woods in the Cumberland Valley, just like my other favorite place, the white sugar sand beaches in the Gulf Coast of Florida.'*"

He looked up at Faith, and she could see the effect it had on him.

"What are you telling me?"

"Somehow, Faith, we have to do both. We have to celebrate what came before us, and then we need to make it all new again. We have to make new magic and add it to the mix. I don't think you have to choose between living by the water and living here. Both places are special. Both places satisfy different needs. It's like the example of your granny. She had two lovers in her life, and she was able to see that that was perfect. And it was."

"You mean it is."

He laughed. "Okay, time for bed."

She put away her books and said goodnight as he headed down the hall to the bedroom with his two friends. Her mom and dad were down at the home making sure the trees had gotten delivered and the staff was aware of what was happening. The boys had been out helping some of the grounds crew fulfill orders so that the party could take place without Faith's parents having to run back to solve problems at the ranch.

There were presents stacked up all over the front porch, things that had been mailed from all over. But as she watched him walk down the hallway, his back to her, she thought about her grandmother. And she thought about how lucky Granny was to fall in love. She was the example of taking a chance on something that was perhaps not something everyone would do. But she did it. And she did it with courage, and she did it with her eyes wide open.

Faith called out to Daniel. He turned and smiled but waited for her to speak.

"Would you sleep with me tonight, Daniel? In this old rickety farmhouse that's seen so much? Would you show me how to make love to you?"

Of course, the answer was yes, but he didn't say anything. He ran to her, grabbed her, closed the door behind, and started ripping off his clothes like crazy.

Then he tossed Faith on the bed.

Whatever was coming next, she was game for it. She was a full participant. She was never going to stop living fully. That was her heritage. It wasn't doing the right thing or being a good girl. It was living her life to the fullest, inspiring others. Faith knew that. Even if her parents didn't understand, Granny surely would.

Chapter 24

Annie Karr

SWEET ROMANCE AUTHOR

F AITH AND DANIEL took James and I over to the old house, and immediately, he took to the property. He ran throughout the main floor and then gingerly climbed the stairs where we could hear him whooping and hollering about the bedrooms upstairs. Daniel couldn't contain himself and ran up to join him.

That left Faith and me in the kitchen, looking out at the overgrown backyard area and what had been my flower garden.

"You remember?"

"I do, Granny. It was lovely. The best place on earth."

I brushed away the tears at seeing the house as it used to look with the furniture, children's artwork, quilts, and the library filled with books Frank used to like reading. In my mind, I could still see his high-back reading chair, and in those days as we were arranging the move, the wool slippers and blanket I used to wrap around his legs. We didn't have a fireplace in the study. We always talked about it, maybe getting a plug-in type, but never did anything about it.

"Seeing it in this condition, I don't have the same reaction as James does. I'm glad he can see the potential. I've lived here and loved this house. Been loved in this house. My time here is done."

"Well, now you have the beach, Granny. You have the beautiful beach and all that space going out to the horizon," she said.

"You're right, of course. Time moves on. This house should go to another owner. Perhaps someday you and Daniel could live here."

Faith blushed. "Not at that stage yet, but there definitely is a connection. I like him, Grandma."

"And that's the most important. You have to like being around each other. You come at it from different points, but the overall effect is you make each other feel better just being around each other. That's a rare thing, something only true love can bring. Nothing is forced about being in love. Even when you have to make do with your own mistakes."

"You didn't make any mistakes, Granny."

I laughed at that. "Let's just leave it at I was good at cleaning things up. I did that out of love too."

I don't think she totally understood me, but that wasn't necessary. The men returned. James looked like he was twenty-five again. It was a blessing to see. He was panting, out of breath, and still a hunk of a man at eighty-five. I prayed he still saw me as twenty.

"There's so much you could do here, Becca. This place is crying for attention," he said.

Daniel was equally as excited. "See, that's what I've been saying. This place could be fabulous if you fixed it up. It needs a lot of work, but really, it's in pretty good shape. These timbers, these hand-hewn beams, you can't buy that anymore," Daniel added enthusiastically.

"What is it? Does this place make you sad?" James asked, observing my reserved behavior. Always a quick read to my moods and my needs, of course.

"There's a lot here nobody but me sees. There are others here, and it's quite overwhelming."

"Tell us. Tell us about it, Granny," asked Faith.

"Oh, Child, I'm not sure—"

James took me in his arms, shielding me from a shiver I'd just felt running up my spine. "It's okay. You don't have to. It's just that to me, it's all new. I'd love to hear it."

Nestled in his arms, I opened the cabinets and started with the kitchen.

"My mother's bowls were here, right where I could

reach them. Faith, you have those bowls now, remember?"

"I do."

"The oven was always on, it seemed. Your little brother had an insatiable appetite for brownies and pies. When you'd visit, I always made it a point to make sure when he walked in he smelled them cooking. I remember washing dishes with you, Faith, and how you were so careful with my plates."

"That's because my mother used plastic ones that wouldn't break."

"Oh, she broke a lot of plates here in this kitchen over the years she lived here. She wasn't the cook you've become, Faith, but she was helpful with the chores and loved to pick flowers and bring them in to me. We had vases here," I pointed to the windowsill looking out into the back over the sink, still with the round stains of jars of flowers left there too long on the ledge, "and here. She even picked weeds sometimes, not knowing."

I walked down past the pantry hallway to the dining room with the big picture windows viewing out to my flower garden and the vegetable garden on the lower plot near the driveway approach. All of this had been and was still surrounded by tall trees waving in the breeze.

"I can't believe these windows have lasted so long. They were horribly expensive to replace. Your dad helped Frank do it, and I'd never heard so much swearing from my otherwise gentleman husband."

I glanced over my shoulder to make sure James wasn't offended. He was crying. I couldn't read him, but no one asked me to stop, so I continued.

"We had lots of family dinners here. Townspeople would come by sometimes for Sunday supper, which was kind of our time to get acquainted with the locals Frank helped. It was one of those Sunday suppers where your mother met your father, Faith. I'd have to say they carried on the tradition of love at first sight."

Faith blushed. "From what I hear, he was her first and only boyfriend."

"It was the right time for both of you. We all know about timing, don't we?" I wouldn't look at anyone for fear I'd see something I didn't want to.

Suddenly, the house came alive, and I saw little Maggie, not more than five, bringing in a butterfly she'd found in the garden, except she was holding it by the wings, and I showed her the proper way to hold him. I took her chubby little hand, extended her forefinger, and let the poor captured Monarch climb on it and then continue onto the back of her hand.

"Let's go set him free, shall we?" I asked her.

Slowly, with her hand outstretched, with my hands on her shoulders, I led her outside to the flower garden.

"This is his home. This is where he belongs."

And then when he flapped his wings, I noticed he wasn't a male but a beautiful female Monarch, large and very sturdy.

"Oh, Maggie, it's a girl! She wants to lay some eggs for you so you can see her babies soon. Isn't that nice?"

Maggie's little face had lit up with such brightness only a child can make. A gentle wind came up, and our Monarch flew off, stopping to rest here and there on my sweet williams, snapdragons, coreopsis, and milkweed. I stood beside her, holding her hand as she observed the wonder of life.

I closed my eyes, and when I opened them, I heard Frank calling to me from the study. Walking through the glass doors to the living room, I crossed it over the rich burgundy rug my grandmother had given me and heard the clock that my father made from a kit chiming.

I opened the doors to the study. Frank was cold. His book had fallen. He'd also dropped his glasses, and he was shivering. I looked at his ashen face and realized that time was drawing to an end for us. I dared not show my emotions or thoughts. His image faded, and I began to cry silently.

This time, it was Faith who wrapped her arms around me. "I remember, Granny. I remember it all."

Daniel looked worried. "Should we go?" His enthusiasm had waned.

James smiled at me lovingly, his right hand over his heart as if he'd felt it, maybe seen it all as well. The intimacy I felt with and for him extended to our past, our dreams and aspirations, the things we chose to remember and the things we left behind for whatever reason. It was the reason I could kiss his older body and remember the man I'd always loved, and he could feel my love for the other man I'd loved as well.

He stepped forward.

"I'm looking at the house you raised our daughter in, that you raised your children in, a house that you were happy in for, what, forty-five years more?"

I was so in love with him I just couldn't even talk. "It was a beautiful home, filled with lots of love. I think it would be wonderful to fix it up for someone else to create happy memories in."

I purposely didn't look at Daniel or Faith, not wanting to embarrass them. And then I had an idea.

"Tell me. Tell me what you'd do," I asked the men.

Daniel spoke up first. "I love it. I mean, this place is fabulous. You could completely refinish the floors. We could put a brand-new kitchen in here. The master needs its own bath, so you could sacrifice one of the bedrooms and make a huge master suite, you know?"

I laughed. "Go on."

"The windows are good, as you said. Inside walls need to be re-plastered. We need to upgrade the electrical, add extra plugs with charging outlets, and put in some 4-gang plugs with grounds. I'm sure it will need a new roof and gutters."

"Oh, yes, the back door... When you went out into the rain, we always got a neck full of drips going out to the garden. Very exciting, but something we should have fixed long ago." Frank had never been very handy in this department, and money was always an issue. If we couldn't do it or make it ourselves, it got left undone.

"Exactly. New gutters!" Daniel said enthusiastically. "You need a new barn, a storage building for feed, supplies for the garden, a firepit—you have so much lumber here, you'd never have to buy firewood—an outdoor kitchen."

"You'd do that too?" I asked, surprised.

"Sort of like a built-in barbeque, really. But if you're canning things or grilling things, you know, outdoors like everyone used to do so it didn't heat up the house too much in the summer when all the fruits and vegetables are ripe!"

I pointed to Daniel. "He's amazing."

Even James laughed along with Faith. Daniel was clearly embarrassed.

"I'm overwhelmed," he admitted. "It's so beautiful, the whole property. You need orchards here. There are trees that look like they produced, but they've been allowed to overgrow, and they haven't been pruned for five or six years, I'd say."

"Faith, he knows his trees too."

Daniel wasn't going to stop. "They may not come back. But we could put good trees here that would grow, and most of all, you could grow grapes here. The exposure is perfect. You have a southern exposure, light, warm afternoons here. It's perfect for grapes."

I had to bring up the realities of the situation. "I'm afraid, though, the family doesn't have money for any of this. But if you want to fix it up, you and James, you have my permission, as long as Margaret and Noel approve, but I doubt there are any available funds for it. That's the biggest problem.

"So it's settled, Becca. Are you in agreement?" James said, his bright blue eyes brighter than the sky at Sunset Beach.

"But the money—"

"Forget the money. I'll bankroll it." He came over

to me, pulled me into his arms. "I'll consider it payment for services rendered before and in the future," he said in his raspy, sexy tone.

I turned to the group. "Now you see? I could never refuse him. Silver-tongued devil of a man I love. Never could ever say no to him."

Of course, I was in agreement, and I let them know. I watched the two men walk through the house making notes, getting inspired by each other's energy. It wasn't something I ever thought I'd see.

Faith was flabbergasted. She also thought it was a good idea, and she asked me, "Who's going to live here?"

"Well, we'll come and visit. But I thought maybe you and Daniel... What do you think, Faith? Could you live here and raise a family here, like I did?"

"He hasn't asked me, Granny."

"I think he will. But even if not, could you live here? Live here and help your parents with the ranch? Be the home's caretaker like you took care of me? It would be like doing that, if you could hold it for me to visit. Like I used to do for you when you'd visit."

"I could. I would do that for you."

I noticed a small hesitation in her voice. "What is it, Child?"

"I have to be honest with you, Granny, I love the

beach. I love Florida. I don't know if I could live here all the time. But Daniel has told me he could do both, as long as he can do a nursery or ranching. He wants to make things grow, work the land."

"Well, we'll fix that too. I think you should come stay at our house in Sunset Beach every year for a certain amount of time. I'd like you to do that. James and I can travel, and we'd leave the house to you for that period of time. That way you can feel like you're not giving up something you love. You may find out that, after a few years, Tennessee is really your home. I don't believe in just having one solution, and it's obvious from the way I've lived my life. It served me well, though. You do one thing that makes sense while it makes sense, and then you do the other thing later."

Faith laughed.

"Oh, silly, I don't mean different husbands. I mean, you live your life as best you can where it makes sense, for lots of reasons, economics, the people you love, the people you support, the people you need to help and be around, but you never give up your dreams. Then there comes a time when you have the opportunity to do something else, something new. And if you tell yourself you can't do it, then you stay small. If you try it, you live large. And living large is where it's at. I honestly think so. I'm going to make sure that we allow one month a year at the beach where you can have the cottage, and that gives us the opportunity to do something different as well, to travel."

"Daniel loves this land, and I know he'd love working with my father."

"Yes, and he was made to be a rancher, Faith."

She knew I was telling her the truth. I wondered if she realized it yet. But when she looked back at me with that glimmer in her eye, I saw it. I saw the miracle starting to grow.

I gathered her to me and gave her a soft hug. "Way too many things to decide now. Just keep an open mind, Faith. And don't be afraid to live."

THE PARTY WAS going to be fabulous. It was awkward for me to stay at the home, the place where I had resided with Frank for so many years, but that was the way it was. Almost as if we were newlyweds and couldn't talk to each other before we got married, James stayed at the ranch and I stayed at the home for those few days until the big event. That made the coming together again so fabulous.

I was able to witness the continued transformation of the large ballroom and felt the excitement of the catering and hired decorating staff James had put together, working with Faith.

I wore the brightest colored dress I could find. Sally had taken me shopping, and this dress looked like it came right out of my old flower garden. Bright tropical flowers just like I'd seen at so many botanical gardens in Florida were all over the material. I had low slippers so I could dance, and my cousins on my mother's side had a little jazz combo that was playing music when we walked in, together.

There were already about fifty people there, a lot of staff, and some patients as well, but when James and I walked in, him in his gold-braided vest which he insisted on, his white pants, his white hair back at a ponytail, I know everyone who knew me was shocked. He was Prince Charming. He was the handsomest man at eighty-five-years old that ever walked or danced on this floor, and I mean ever.

And that's what we did. We listened to music, we laughed, we talked to all our friends, and we even got to see Savannah and Penny, who flew in for the event. There were so many new people I had to introduce him to.

He was the life of the party, listening to all the stories in rapt attention. It was like he'd been here with me all along. I'd never seen him laugh so much, and nobody, even Frank's relatives who attended, asked me the big question. If they had, the answer, of course, was yes. Yes, I missed Frank dearly, and in some kind of way, I wished he could've been there. He would've enjoyed it. Afterall, he gave me the life I needed to survive perhaps a horrible decision with a miraculous outcome. He made it possible. Without his love, this life of mine would never have happened.

I even danced with Noel, who was all left feet, frustrated with himself, and I had to laugh.

"What do you think about your new father-in-law?"

"Well, I still consider Frank my father-in-law."

"Of course, you do. And I wouldn't have it any other way. But I'll tell you a secret. He's a softie. He's very easy to love, and he has a huge heart. He doesn't want you not to love Frank. He wants you to love Frank and me, and he makes me happy."

"I think you must have given your parents quite a run. I kind of understand now what your parents were talking about when I married Maggie. I'll never forget it. He said to me, your dad, he said to me, 'Noel, it's going to be the hardest job you've ever had, and you'll never regret it.'"

That thrilled me.

"We've made an agreement, James and I, that the kids are welcome if they'd like to come out to Florida and spend a while at the house, that we'll let them stay for a while if they want."

"That sounds very generous of you. They'd love to,

I know."

"Good, I'm glad you approve. I know that you're planning on having these boys help you with the ranch. James and I have talked about it, and he has no heirs, so we'd like to give the house at Sunset Beach to you and Maggie when we're done. I want you to keep it there for all of you to use, for all of you to feel the magic that lives there, that comes from the beach. Will you do that?"

"We'd be honored."

I danced until I got blisters on my feet. I drank a little bit too much too. I let the love of my life pick me up and carry me to the woods. He'd laid out a blanket for me, and under the stars and under the whispering trees of the woods in the house I'd been happy in, far from the ocean and far from the beach after all those years, I still loved the touch of his hands on my body. My body was eighty years old.

But when he touched me, I felt twenty and he was twenty-five.

Ready for more Annie Carr stories? Be sure to pick up Book 2, a standalone, **Back To You**.

ABOUT THE AUTHOR

The Sweet Romance sister penname for NYT-USA Today best-selling author Sharon Hamilton, Annie Carr steps through the pages of one of Sharon's Sunset SEALs books as one of her heroines.

Based on Sharon's character Aimee Carr in SEALed At Sunset and The House At Sunset Beach, Annie lives her life on the Florida Gulf Coast, composing her novels in a house that once ignited the love affair between a famous science fiction writer afflicted with writer's block and a young woman looking to find herself on the white sugar-sand beaches. Her women's romantic fiction stories will melt your heart and leave the bedroom to your own imagination!

She believes in long, slow kisses and walks on the beach at sunset, the warm surf between her toes as she searches for shells and colorful pieces of sea glass, thinking up stories she'd like to read.

Afterall, the beach does heal everything.

She loves hearing from her fans:
Sharonhamilton2001@gmail.com

Her website is:
sharonhamiltonauthor.com

Find out more about Annie Carr, her upcoming releases, appearances and news when you sign up for Annie Carr's newsletter.

Facebook:
facebook.com/SharonHamiltonAuthor

Twitter:
twitter.com/sharonlhamilton

Pinterest:
pinterest.com/AuthorSharonH

Amazon:
amazon.com/Sharon-Hamilton/e/B004FQQMAC

BookBub:
bookbub.com/authors/sharon-hamilton

Youtube:
youtube.com/channel/UCDInkxXFpXp_4Vnq08ZxMBQ

Soundcloud:
soundcloud.com/sharon-hamilton-1

Annie Carr's Rockin' Romance Readers:
facebook.com/groups/sealteamromance

Annie Carr's Goodreads Group:
goodreads.com/group/show/199125-sharon-hamilton-readers-group

Visit Annie Carr's Online Store:
sharon-hamilton-author.myshopify.com

Join Annie Carr's Review Teams:

eBook Reviews:
sharonhamiltonassistant@gmail.com

Audio Reviews:
sharonhamiltonassistant@gmail.com

Life is one fool thing after another.
Love is two fool things after each other.

REVIEWS

PRAISE FOR THE
GOLDEN VAMPIRES OF TUSCANY SERIES

"Well to say the least I was thoroughly surprise. I have read many Vampire books, from Ann Rice to Kym Grosso and few other Authors, so yes I do like Vampires, not the super scary ones from the old days, but the new ones are far more interesting far more human than one can remember. I found Honeymoon Bite a totally engrossing book, I was not able to put it down, page after page I found delight, love, understanding, well that is until the bad bad Vamp started being really bad. But seeing someone love another person so much that they would do anything to protect them, well that had me going, then well there was more and for a while I thought it was the end of a beautiful love story that spanned not only time but, spanned Italy and California. Won't divulge how it ended, but I did shed a few tears after screaming but Sharon Hamilton did not let me down, she took me on amazing trip that I loved, look forward to reading another Vampire book of hers."

"An excellent paranormal romance that was exciting, romantic, entertaining and very satisfying to read. It had me anticipating what would happen next many times over, so much so I could not put it down and even finished it up in a day. The vampires in this book were different from your average vampire, but I enjoy different variations and changes to the same old stuff. It made for a more unpredictable read and more adventurous to explore! Vampire lovers, any paranormal readers and even those who love the romance genre will enjoy Honeymoon Bite."

"This is the first non-Seal book of this author's I have read and I loved it. There is a cast-like hierarchy in this vampire community with humans at the very bottom and Golden vampires at the top. Lionel is a dark vampire who are servants of the Goldens. Phoebe is a Golden who has not decided if she will remain human or accept the turning to become a vampire. Either way she and Lionel can never be together since it is forbidden.

I enjoyed this story and I am looking forward to the next installment."

"A hauntingly romantic read. Old love lost and new love found. Family, heart, intrigue and vampires. Grabbed my attention and couldn't put down. Would definitely recommend."

REVIEWS

PRAISE FOR THE
SEAL BROTHERHOOD SERIES

"Fans of Navy SEAL romance, I found a new author to feed your addiction. Finely written and loaded delicious with moments, Sharon Hamilton's storytelling satisfies like a thick bar of chocolate." —Marliss Melton, bestselling author of the *Team Twelve* Navy SEALs series

"Sharon Hamilton does an EXCELLENT job of fitting all the characters into a brotherhood of SEALS that may not be real but sure makes you feel that you have entered the circle and security of their world. The stories intertwine with each book before...and each book after and THAT is what makes Sharon Hamilton's SEAL Brotherhood Series so very interesting. You won't want to put down ANY of her books and they will keep you reading into the night when you should be sleeping. Start with this book...and you will not want to stop until you've read the whole series and then...you will be waiting for Sharon to write the next one." (5 Star Review)

"Kyle and Christy explode all over the pages in this first book, *[Accidental SEAL]*, in a whole new series of SEALs. If the twist and turns don't get your heart jumping, then maybe the suspense will. This is a must read for those that are looking for love and adventure with a little sloppy love thrown in for good measure." (5 Star Review)

PRAISE FOR THE
BAD BOYS OF SEAL TEAM 3 SERIES

"I love reading this series! Once you start these books, you can hardly put them down. The mix of romance and suspense keeps you turning the pages one right after another! Can't wait until the next book!" (5 Star Review)

"I love all of Sharon's Seal books, but *[SEAL's Code]* may just be her best to date. Danny and Luci's journey is filled with a wonderful insight into the Native American life. It is a love story that will fill you with warmth and contentment. You will enjoy Danny's journey to become a SEAL and his reasons for it. Good job Sharon!" (5 Star Review)

PRAISE FOR THE
BAND OF BACHELORS SERIES

"*[Lucas]* was the first book in the Band of Bachelors series and it was a phenomenal start. I loved how we got to see the other SEALs we all love and we got a look at Lucas and Marcy. They had an instant attraction, and their love was very intense. This book had it all, suspense, steamy romance, humor, everything you want in a riveting, outstanding read. I can't wait to read the next book in this series." (5 Star Review)

PRAISE FOR THE
TRUE BLUE SEALS SERIES

"Keep the tissues box nearby as you read *True Blue SEALs: Zak* by Sharon Hamilton. I imagine more than I wish to that the circumstances surrounding Zak and Amy are all too real for returning military personnel and their families. Ms. Hamilton has put us right in the middle of struggles and successes that these two high school sweethearts endure. I have read several of Sharon Hamilton's military romances but will say this is the most emotionally intense of the ones that I have read. This is a well-written, realistic story with authentic characters that will have you rooting for them and proud of those who serve to keep us safe. This is an author who writes amazing stories that you love and cry with the characters. Fans of Jessica Scott and Marliss Melton will want to add Sharon Hamilton to their list of realistic military romance writers." (5 Star Review)

Made in the USA
Columbia, SC
08 June 2023

17737708R00143